In Search of a Sandhill Crane

In Search of a Sandhill Crane

KEITH ROBERTSON

Illustrated by Richard Cuffari

THE VIKING PRESS   NEW YORK

In Search of a Sandhill Crane

1

The big plane had to wait a few minutes at the end of the take-off strip. Lincoln Keller sat looking out of the plane window at the airport building, wondering if his mother were watching or if she had gone home. How had it all happened? Had he actually decided that he wanted to go to Michigan, or had he just drifted with the idea so long that it became impossible to back out? Half a dozen times he had been on the verge of admitting that the thought of going way off into the wilds of Michigan was not only uninviting but half scared him. He'd gone camping twice at a Scout camp, and both times had been disastrous. Once it had rained the entire week, and he had been damp and cold and had developed a terrible cough. The second time he had wrenched his ankle the first day and had spent a lonely week hobbling around camp while everyone else was off on various expeditions.

He had a great deal of pride, and according to his mother his pride was often mixed with stubbornness. He hadn't wanted to admit that all his talk about Michigan was mere bravado and that he didn't want to go. As a result there he was, about to fly off hundreds of miles from home when he was already half homesick.

Link's father had died when he was a small boy, and Link's mother, Rebecca, had worked as a bookkeeper since. She was a capable, hard-working woman, and her firm had picked her to take a ten-weeks' course in computer operation. That meant she would be in Ohio most of the summer. She was pleased and excited at the prospect, and it meant a sizable increase in salary, which she could use. Link was proud of his mother and glad that she would have an unusual and interesting summer, but his plans were certainly a mess as a result. For some years they had rented a cottage at the New Jersey seashore for several weeks in August. He would miss the Shore and the friends he usually met there. Months earlier he had invited Pedro Ortiz, his best friend, to spend the vacation with them, and now he would have to withdraw the invitation. He had lined up a part-time job for most of July. It paid well and was only two blocks away, but now he couldn't take it. Finally, he and Pedro had organized a neighborhood baseball team, which would now be playing without him. He'd suggested staying home by himself, but his mother hadn't thought much of the idea.

"What would you eat? You'd live off sardine sandwiches and soda and you'd stay up half the night. I know you think nothing could happen to you, but I couldn't go off and leave a fifteen-year-old son of mine to shift for himself all summer."

"I'll be sixteen early in July," Link had pointed out.

Mrs. Keller conceded the point with a shrug of her shoulders. "If I left you all by yourself, I'd worry so that I wouldn't be able to study."

Link knew that she would, too. He hadn't argued too long, partly because he knew it was useless and partly because the idea of a summer alone, doing all his own cooking, wasn't too attractive. There was no problem about places he could go. The trouble was that he could go to too many.

Rebecca Keller had three sisters, all married. None of them had children still living at home, hence Link was thought of as "the baby" of the entire clan. All his aunts and uncles were fond of him and wanted to have him for the summer. This had been the principal topic of conversation at a Sunday dinner at Link's house.

"The logical thing is for him to come to our house for the summer," his Aunt Louise had said with finality. "We have a big house with lots of room, and we'd love to have him. We have five bedrooms, you know, and a game room where he could entertain his friends."

"We all know you have a big house," Alice Cooke said. "He'd rattle around in it like a pea in a pod. The trouble with your house is that it's in too swank a neighborhood. Everyone around you has money enough to send his children off to camp. There'd be no one Link's age and you know it. He'd die of boredom."

"We expect to go up to the cabin in the Adirondacks for the last ten days in July and about half of August," Louise Stern said, helping herself to more food. "Link would enjoy the mountains."

"I think he'd be much happier at our place," Marjorie Wolfe said. "You'd like Wantagh, Link. And while the surfing on Long Island may not be as good as it is along the Jersey coast, I know you'd prefer the water any day to the mountains."

"I think he should try something completely different and spend the summer with us," Alice Cooke persisted. Alice and Simon Cooke lived in an apartment in Peter Cooper Village in New York City. She worked in a department store and Simon taught music.

"I don't know how different that would be, but it would certainly be hotter," Louise Stern had said. "I can hardly bear to go into the city to shop during the summer."

"Most places are air conditioned," Alice pointed out. "And a boy Link's age and weight doesn't mind the heat. There're a thousand things to do in the city. Dozens of museums that Link's never been near, and Si can get him passes to all sorts of concerts. He's old enough to get a great deal out of a summer in New York. It can be a great cultural experience, you know. And with

Link as interested in art as he is, he'd enjoy himself tremendously. I can probably find a summer course in art if he'd like."

Link liked to draw and was reasonably good at it. But he was not at all certain that he wanted to spend his summer going to art classes or walking through museums. He enjoyed museums in small doses, but they always made his feet hurt almost as much as being dragged along when his mother shopped in a department store.

They continued to argue heatedly and noisily about his summer. Only Albert Wolfe was quiet. He was always quiet. He was a small, bespectacled little man who sat smiling quietly as though amused at the noise and talk swirling around him. He seldom joined the discussions. Link sometimes wondered if Uncle Albert listened either. Perhaps he was off in the clouds occupied with thoughts of his own. Link often was himself, but that afternoon, since the subject concerned him, he had listened.

Everyone seemed to have forgotten that he had any opinion. No one asked what he'd like to do. He became more and more annoyed as the argument went on. While he liked all his aunts and uncles, and he knew they really wanted him to visit them for the summer, he didn't think he'd have much fun with any of them.

"I guess we'd better divide him up," Herbert Stern announced with a chuckle. "Do a King Solomon. Each of us take him for a third of the time."

Link was afraid that would be the final solution. Then

all three families would get a chance to practice their child-rearing theories on him. He started to comment that he thought *he* should have something to say about his summer, but he stopped just in time. Someone was certain to ask him what he sugegsted, and he didn't have any suggestions. Where else could he go? Then he had thought of his Aunt Harriet. Harriet Keller was his father's only sister, and she lived in Michigan. Link remembered her vaguely from a short visit five or six years earlier. She was tall, thin, and had seemed cold and forbidding to a boy used to a warm, bubbling person like Rebecca Keller. Link's mother and his Aunt Harriet kept in touch with occasional letters. When Mrs. Keller had written that she would be away at school for the summer, Aunt Harriet had invited Link to come visit her in Michigan. She had written Link a separate note which he had not yet answered.

DEAR LINCOLN:

I still have the small cabin on the Upper Peninsula that your grandparents bought years ago. Your father went there a number of summers as a boy. Since they have built the bridge, the Upper Peninsula is not quite so wild and isolated as it once was. I'm not sure whether that is good or bad. One always wants to be the only tourist, I guess, and resents all the others who are looking for the same peace and quiet. Anyhow, we could go up to the cabin if you'd like, and you could have a look at the wilderness before it vanishes.

I would enjoy having you very much. You are my
only close relative, and it would be nice to get to
know you. I promise not to hover over you if you
come.

WITH LOVE,
Aunt Harriet

Link had not even considered the idea of going to
Michigan, but at least the invitation gave him a choice
that he could talk about. There had been a sudden lull
in the conversation. Mrs. Keller got up to get the dessert.

"I've been thinking about going to Michigan," Link
had said, making the remark as off-hand as he could.

The lull lengthened into a long silence of absolute
astonishment. All his aunts and uncles stared at him in
amazement, and his mother stopped halfway to the
kitchen and stood frozen. Link smiled inwardly. He had
really shaken them up. He sat back in his chair and tried
to look unconcerned.

"What's in Michigan?" Alice Cooke asked in a puzzled voice. "Why would you go there?"

"Link's Aunt Harriet," Rebecca said, looking thoughtfully at her son. "She invited him to come spend the
summer with her."

"Oh yes, she teaches school doesn't she? She was here
to visit some years back," Marjorie Wolfe said.

"Six years ago," Rebecca said. "We were out to your
house for lunch."

"She seemed very nice, as I remember," Alice Cooke said. Her vague look showed that she did not remember Harriet Keller at all. "But what on earth would one do all summer in a place like Michigan? Why, that's where they make all the cars. You'd either get killed on the highway or die of boredom, Link."

"Harriet Keller lives near Saginaw," Albert said to no one in particular. "Central Michigan, not too far from Crawford County."

There was another surprised pause. Albert so seldom entered the conversation that everyone listened when he did.

"How do you happen to know that bit of surprising information?" Alice Cooke asked.

"Kirtland's warbler," Albert Wolfe said mildly. "The first Kirtland's warbler nest ever found was in Crawford County, Michigan. It's a very rare species, and it nests only in a small area. I talked to Harriet about it when she was here. She's seen several of them."

Albert Wolfe was a bird watcher. He kept a book and carefully recorded each species that he identified. He spent much of his spare time seated in his large back yard in Wantagh, where he had erected at least six bird feeders that he kept filled winter and summer. According to his wife, he put out enough feed each year to feed half the entire bird population of Long Island, and only two varieties ever visited—sparrows and starlings. Albert simply smiled to himself and went on feeding and watching the birds.

"That will give you something to do all summer, Link," Alice Cooke said dryly. "You can look for a Kirtland's warbler."

"Keep your eyes open and you might see a tufted nightshirt or a double-breasted seersucker," Herbert Stern said and then laughed loudly at his own joke.

"I've never been to Michigan," Link said. "It would be fun to go some place new." He got to his feet to help his mother bring dessert in from the kitchen.

Rebecca Keller followed her son into the kitchen. "Ohio is right below Michigan," she said quietly. "If you really do decide to go there, I might be able to get up to see you once or twice."

Link was pleased. He must have been convincing. Even his mother thought he was serious about Michigan.

They returned to the table and served the dessert. Conversation still lagged as everyone digested the idea that Link might go to Michigan for the summer.

"Won't you be bored out there?" Alice Cooke asked finally, in a faintly annoyed voice. "You like to sketch things and take pictures. What is there to draw out there? Cows?"

"Kirtland's warbler," Herbert Stern said with a chuckle.

"A man named Audubon drew a few birds," Albert Wolfe said. "His work is considered art, I believe."

"Much of Michigan is very beautiful," Herbert Stern said, becoming serious. "Louise and I drove up over that long bridge to what they call the Upper Peninsula. Remember that Louise—we went on to Canada? That's really wild country up there. Bears, wolves, moose, trees, lakes, and swamps. Get ten feet off the highway and you could be back in the days of the Indians. That Upper Peninsula is wilderness."

"That's where I'm going," Link had said as though it were all settled. "Aunt Harriet has a cabin up there. She says my father used to go there as a boy."

"Ugh!" Alice Cooke said with a shudder. "Mosquitoes, flies, snakes, and things that creep around in the night. You can have it!"

The conversation turned to other subjects, and finally the dinner and coffee were over. Link helped clear the table and then went upstairs to his room to read. Half an hour later his uncle Albert poked his head in the door.

"I'd like to talk to you a minute," he said hesitantly.

"Come on in," Link invited. He got up from the one chair and sat on the bed.

"I know you like to take pictures," Albert said. "And you've taken some good ones. Most of those I've seen have been taken at your school or here in Nutley. You seem to like people in your photographs."

"I hadn't thought about it, but I guess I do like to photograph people," Link said. "When they don't know you're taking them, mainly."

"Well, if you spend much time up on that Upper Peninsula, you might be short of subjects," Albert said.

"You might want to take some shots of wild animals and birds. It takes a lot of patience to take a good picture of a bird, but I've found it a lot of fun."

"I might try it," Link said, wondering what his uncle had in mind.

"You'll need the right equipment," Albert said. "Lots of time the light is poor, and you need a good lens and fast film. I thought if you were interested, I would lend you my camera and equipment for the summer."

Link had been lounging back on his pillow. Now he sat bolt upright. His uncle Albert had a very expensive camera with a large assortment of lenses. He also had a magnificent collection of slides of various birds that he had taken over the years. Link had sat through showings of them at least five times on visits to the Wolfes.

Albert was a fussy, meticulous man, and he always kept his camera equipment in an aluminum case the size of a small suitcase. It was lined with sponge rubber with a cutout for each lens, filter, or other piece of equipment. Link had talked with his uncle about technical details of photography a number of times and knew that he was an expert. He also knew that Albert had never before allowed anyone to borrow or even touch his equipment. It was unbelievable.

"Gee, thanks, but I'd be worried something might happen to some of it," Link said.

"What could happen to it?" Albert asked. "You're a responsible boy, and you know enough about photography that you know how to take care of equipment. Besides, you'd have my carrying case and everything is pretty safe in that. I've got insurance against theft and fire and things like that."

Link gulped. Albert meant everything since he was offering the entire case. Suppose I scratched a lens?" Link said doubtfully. "I'd have to work all year to pay for it."

"You won't scratch anything,' Albert Wolfe said quietly. "Think it over. There're two cameras, you know. One I use only for close-ups. You might not want to bother with that. You're a city boy, and a summer in the country may seem a little slow at first. Taking some pictures might help pass away the time. If you decide to take the equipment, there's one thing I'd like you to do for me."

"What's that?" Link asked. Albert Wolfe must want something very much to be willing to lend his precious photographic equipment.

"Get me some pictures of a sandhill crane," Albert said. "They do a crazy dance, jumping up in the air and bowing. I'd love to have some pictures of that."

"Well, I could try," Link said. "I've never photographed a bird."

"Nothing to it," Albert said with a slight smile. "Just takes plenty of patience and plenty of film. Don't be afraid of using film. If you make fifty exposures and get just one good picture, you're doing all right with wild animals and birds. Now here's twenty dollars. It's best to buy fresh film as you need it. If you run out of money, write me for more. All I ask is a good color slide of a sandhill crane."

That was how the idea of a summer in Michigan had begun. He had planned to wait a few days and then announce he had decided not to go. The trouble was that he had enjoyed all the excitement his proposed trip had caused, and he had delayed too long. It was his own fault, he admitted, as he waited glumly for the plane to take off. He had been working up to telling his mother it was all a mistake, when she came home one day and announced that she had written to Harriet Keller during her lunch hour.

"I didn't say definitely that you were coming, but I did say you would like to if she didn't think having you would be too much work and trouble. After all, we do have to let her know that there is a possibility. She has to make plans. I checked the air fare from Cleveland—I'll be staying near there—and it's not too much. It's just as I thought. I might be able to fly up to see you." Mrs. Keller was busy getting dinner and had her back turned toward her son.

Lincoln cleared his throat to say that he had changed his mind, but before he could get out the first word, his mother continued.

"I'm glad that you decided to go to Michigan in a way," she said. "You haven't really been much of anywhere, and seeing another part of the country will do you good. Lots of boys your age wouldn't do it—they'd be afraid of being homesick."

After that Link decided he would wait until he could think up a good reason why he had changed his mind. He hadn't found one by Sunday afternoon when his Uncle Albert came by with his case full of cameras and lenses. He spent two hours explaining how to operate everything and talking about the finer points of taking pictures of birds. Link said feebly at one point that he wasn't absolutely certain that he would go to Michigan, but Albert was so busy talking about his pet hobby that he didn't pay any attention. He kept on talking about shutter speeds and different types of film and what lens to use for what.

"I've never known Albert to trust anyone to use his cameras before," Mrs. Keller said when he had gone. "Not even for a day. He certainly has a lot of faith in you. Why, that equipment is worth a small fortune! Take good care of it now, Link, and get him the picture he wants."

Link had continued to put off doing or saying anything, and finally it was too late. Aunt Harriet wrote that she was delighted that he was coming and wanted to know what plane to meet. And then one day his mother came home with the plane ticket.

"All I did was say I thought I *might* go to Michigan," he had said that night to his friend, Pedro Ortiz, who came by to listen to some records. "And now I'm practically there. It doesn't do to open your mouth around this family."

"Never volunteer for anything," Pedro advised. "That's what my brother in the army says. Ask for something and you're liable to get it. Then you can't complain."

"I can," Link said. "What am I going to do way out in the sticks of Michigan all summer with an old maid aunt?"

"Take pictures of birds," Pedro said, whooping with laughter. "What was that thing? What kind of crane?"

"A sandhill crane," Link said sourly. "You can't spend all summer taking pictures of one crazy bird."

He had grown more and more certain that it was all a big mistake as the time drew nearer but he had been ashamed to admit it. His mother sensed his doubts as she drove him to the airport.

"If you find it hopelessly dull, write me," she said. "I'll try to think of some graceful way out for you. Perhaps I could have Louise write and say Herbert wasn't feeling well and they needed you to help take care of their grounds. But no matter what happens, you have to stay two or three weeks because Harriet has gone to a great deal of trouble, opening the cabin and all that. You don't want to hurt her feelings."

2

Lincoln had flown only once before, and for a while the excitement of take-off gave him a sense of false enthusiasm. This soon wore off. The skies quickly became cloudy, and the plane entered a strange, gray, depressing world. There was nothing to see, and the plane seemed to be making no headway at all but to be suspended in a gray misty void. The seat beside Link was empty, so he had no one to talk to. He stared out the window, feeling less and less enthusiastic with each mile that slid behind him. Finally, as the plane started down in Detroit, he realized that although he had not yet arrived, he was already homesick.

The small two-engine plane to Saginaw had scarcely climbed to its flying altitude before it began its descent to Saginaw. Link waited until he was the last to leave the plane, wondering how he would recognize Aunt

Harriet. He needn't have worried, because the ten or twelve passengers ahead of him went hurrying on their way, leaving one tall elderly woman standing beside the gate. She saw him and raised a hand in a wave of greeting. As Link drew near, he saw that she was using a cane.

"It's wonderful to see you Lincoln," she said in a flat nasal voice, holding out a thin bony hand. "I hope you had a smooth trip."

Link shook his aunt's hand and mumbled something about it being nice to be there. His mother had warned him that Aunt Harriet would probably be undemonstrative, but still he was unprepared. If one of his mother's sisters had met him at an airport, she would have thrown her arms around him, kissed him several times, and have asked him at least six questions without waiting for an answer, ending with wanting to know if he were hungry.

"It's sort of a gray miserable day for flying or driving," Harriet said. "Do you have other luggage?" She glanced at the aluminum case that he was carrying.

"This is camera equipment," Link said. "It belongs to my Uncle Albert. He asked me to get a picture of some bird. It's small enough to stick under my seat, and I thought it would be a good idea if I hung onto it because he'd have a fit if anything happened to his cameras. I checked my bag."

"That's right, your Uncle Albert has a great many

color slides of birds. I saw some that were outstanding. What bird does he want you to photograph?"

"Something called a sandhill crane," Link said. "He says it jumps way up in the air and does a crazy dance. He's got some nice equipment here, and so I've got to get a good picture."

"Sounds interesting," Harriet said with a faint smile. "You're headed for sandhill crane country. They're very interesting birds but very wary. You may have some trouble getting close enough for a really good photograph." She gestured with her cane. "The baggage claim is over this way."

She walked slowly, leaning heavily on her cane. Link had to pause every third step to keep from forging ahead.

"He's got a real neat telescopic lens," he said confidently. "I won't have any trouble." His aunt was probably thinking of some simple little camera that you had to hold within ten feet of the object to get a good picture.

He found his suitcase almost at once. He picked it up and followed his aunt toward the entrance.

"I'm sorry that I can't carry one of those," she said. "And that I'm so slow. Arthritis."

"Is it painful?" Link asked sympathetically.

"At times," she said matter of factly. "But the pain doesn't bother me as much as the thought of the things I can no longer do."

She glanced at the aluminum case he was carrying,

but Link had the feeling that her thoughts were far away. He wondered what it was that she wanted to do but couldn't. Had she been one of his aunts back home he would have asked. That was silly, he decided suddenly. If he was going to spend two weeks with her, he might as well get to know her. Besides, she didn't seem nearly as forbidding as she had in his vague memory of her.

"What is it that you would like to do but can't?"

"Hike through the woods and watch the wild animals and birds," she replied promptly, her face lighting with enthusiasm.

She didn't look as old as he first thought, Link decided. It was that limp that made her seem elderly. Otherwise she looked like a woman who could still hike through the woods. There was a lean, wiry competence about her.

"I detest hearing people talk about their ills," she said. "Including myself. But I thought I'd explain so that when I don't do certain things you'll know it's because I can't."

She led the way across the parking lot toward a Jeep station wagon. Link put his suitcase and camera case in the back seat and climbed in beside his aunt.

"Four-wheel drive, isn't it?" he asked, somewhat surprised.

"Yes, it's handy to get to school on a snowy day. I'm sort of a nervous driver when it's slippery."

It wasn't just when it was slippery, Lincoln thought before they had driven a mile. Harriet sat bolt upright, concentrated fiercely on the road ahead, and sawed back and forth on the wheel, keeping it in constant motion. Her top speed seemed to be forty miles an hour—and that when the road was straight for at least a mile and empty of all cars. When another automobile appeared in the distance, she began to slow down and to ease over to the right. Link was too young to have a driver's license, but he knew he could drive better with his eyes closed than his Aunt Harriet.

"That plane is sometimes late so I didn't plan any dinner," she said, breaking a long silence. "There's a nice place to eat up ahead a few miles. We'll stop there."

The airport seemed to be located in the midst of farm country, but they passed through the outskirts of Midland, Michigan, on the way to Harriet Keller's home. As the number of cars increased, so did Harriet's nervousness. She seemed so intent on the problems of getting past all those threatening cars coming at her that Link was afraid to talk. So he looked around curiously.

He was not certain exactly what he had expected, but the highway seemed to be flanked by the same diners, pizza parlors, frozen custard stands, and service stations as back home. He could, with very little imagination, think that he was back home in northern New Jersey.

"If you get off a plane anywhere in the United States it looks very much the same doesn't it?" she asked, as though she had read his thoughts. "You see the same gas stations, root beer stands, and hamburger places. Oh, I suppose if you got off the plane in Arizona, you might notice cactus instead of maple trees, and the buildings would have a Spanish or warm-country look, but largely everything would be the same. Too many people." She paused a moment and then added, "Now up at the cabin you'll see a difference. That's why I like it."

Link wasn't certain that he wanted to notice a difference. Several of the pizza places looked inviting. He'd like a root beer, for that matter. Aunt Harriet didn't stop. Link suspected she would have thought getting in or out of any of the drive-in places much too dangerous to attempt. Each time a car pulled out into the highway ahead of her, no matter how far away, she drew in her breath sharply and stepped on the brake. Her worry began to affect Link, and he gave a sigh of relief when they finally got back into more or less open countryside again.

They stopped at a restaurant on the outskirts of a tiny town and had dinner. Then they drove on again for another forty-five minutes. It was beginning to grow dark when Harriet announced that the village ahead was Melton, where she lived.

"Melton is a nice quiet little town," she said, "but even it is changing." "That's a drive-in bank." she nodded toward a small brick structure at the edge of town. "Now why would anyone put a bank way out here? It's got a drive-up window where you can do business without getting out of your car. If I were a bank I certainly wouldn't want a bunch of customers who were so lazy they couldn't get out of their cars to put money in their accounts."

Link scarcely had time to look closely at the bank before they were in the center of Melton's business district. This consisted of two blocks of stores, all of which were tightly closed except one. It seemed to be a combination of lunch spot and newsstand.

There was a drugstore, two grocery stores, a hardware store, a dress shop, and what seemed to be a small variety store. He looked for a movie but without success.

"There used to be a movie house, but it burned a few years back and was never rebuilt," Harriet said when he asked. "I guess people watch television. Your father and I were born on a farm about six miles from here, but we moved here when he was a small boy. This is where he lived all his young years."

And probably why he left Michigan and went East, Link thought. What on earth had his father done for excitement in a little burg like this? They hadn't even had television when he was a boy.

Harriet turned down a side street. "That's the high school up there," she said pointing up the street toward a red brick building that looked surprisingly large and modern. "And that little white house up there on the left is us."

Harriet Keller's house was a tiny white bungalow set in the middle of a rather large lot dotted by huge maples. The street was pleasant and shaded and quiet. Much too quiet, Link decided as they got out of the car. Probably no one under sixty lived on it. He got his bags and followed his aunt indoors. They entered through a side door that led into a spotlessly clean kitchen. There was a small living room, a dining room that had been made into a study, two bedrooms, and a bath.

"This is your room," Harriet said, opening the door to one of the bedrooms. "Not that you will get to spend much time in it. I thought we might as well go on up to the cabin tomorrow morning so there's not much point in unpacking." She glanced at Link's bag. "I don't know what you brought. Do you mind if I see? We may have to get you a few things."

Link opened his suitcase and spread it out on a long low chest under the window. Harriet Keller quickly looked through his clothes, scarcely disturbing anything.

"Did you pack that or did Rebecca?" she asked with a small smile.

"Mom did," Link admitted.

"I thought it looked awfully neat," she said dryly. "Well, you might as well hang that nice jacket and those trousers in the closet. And your ties. Put those white shirts in the bureau. Take one on the off-chance you might need it. It's best to take that sweater along. Sometimes it gets cold in the evenings. I'm glad you brought blue jeans, because that's what you'll be wearing. Those knit sport shirts are nice except they have a tendency to snag when you're pushing through the underbrush. I think maybe we'd better stop along the way and get you a pair of hiking boots and a long-sleeved shirt or two. Khaki or denim or something like that."

"Isn't it hot for long sleeves?" Lincoln asked, a bit annoyed at her deciding what he should wear.

"Very," Harriet Keller admitted. "But sometimes it's better to be too hot than all scratched up. Or eaten alive by insects." She finished her quick inventory of his clothes. "You have most everything you need, and in case you don't we'll get to Manistique or Munising now and again. Now I suggest that we go to bed. I'd like to get an early start in the morning. I prefer to drive before the roads get crowded. If we start early enough we can miss all the traffic of people going to work."

Since there was nothing else to do, Lincoln didn't argue about going to bed so early. He went to the bathroom, brushed his teeth, and returned to his room. The bed was comfortable enough, but he couldn't get to sleep. He turned on the light and glanced at his watch. It was still only a few minutes past nine. Pedro would never believe it. Link started framing the letter he would write his friend. "*Out here they roll up the sidewalks at sundown and climb into bed about an hour later. By nine o'clock no one is awake or prowling about except wolves and coyotes. And they have miles and miles of open space all to themselves. I could throw a*

34

baseball from one end of this town to the other." He ran out of things to say to Pedro and started composing the letter he would write his mother asking her to rescue him. He had to stay two weeks to be polite, she had said. It would be a long two weeks if this afternoon was any sample.

It wasn't that Harriet didn't seem glad to have him or wasn't friendly. It was just that he came from a family where people were always doing exciting things and talking about them. What was he going to talk about with Harriet? Well, he would just have to try. He would be polite and do his best to act as though he were enjoying himself. He was wondering what excuse would be best to explain his leaving early when he drifted off to sleep.

When Harriet said an "early start" she meant exactly that. It seemed to Link that he had just closed his eyes when she knocked on the door and called "Lincoln! Lincoln! Time to get up. Breakfast will be ready in about ten minutes."

Link struggled to a sitting position and looked at the window. The world was a dull gray. It must be cloudy and about to rain, he decided sleepily. Then he glanced at his watch. He shook it and then looked at it again. He was right. It was only five thirty! What a horrible shock to a person's nervous system, he thought as he searched for his toothbrush. He could not recall ever having got up at five thirty before in his entire life.

As he returned to his room from the bathroom, he smelled bacon. His aunt must have got up at five o'clock to have breakfast practically cooked. People in Michigan must think they were still pioneers. Or be out of their minds.

There was a pile of boxes, several suitcases, a broom, several buckets, three laundry bags of bedclothes, and a gasoline can sitting beside the kitchen door. "Everything's packed and ready," Harriet said as they ate breakfast. "All we need to do is load it into the station wagon."

Link finished his bacon and eggs. Then while Harriet cleaned off the table and washed the dishes, he packed the station wagon. The space from the tailgate to the back of the front seat was filled when he finished. Harriet Keller did not bother checking that he had got everything or that he had stowed it properly. She simply asked if he had packed everything, and when he said yes, she locked the rear door and climbed into the car.

"Before the roads get crowded" meant "no one else on the road" to Harriet, Link decided. They had driven ten miles before they met their first car. Then they turned onto a superhighway that was almost equally deserted. The broad empty highway stretching off into the distance seemed to give Harriet Keller confidence. She increased her speed to forty-five miles an hour. Link kept looking at the roadside and then the speedometer in disbelief. If the manufacturer had only known, he could have omitted high gear and Harriet would never have noticed the difference. However, even at that speed the countryside began to change. The open fields and farmland began to give way to more and more woods. The maples and hickories began to take second place to evergreens.

"Lots of trees," Link observed after a lengthy silence. Harriet didn't chatter.

"Yes, but there's quite a bit of farming. Much of Michigan is dairy country. Farther north they raise quite a few potatoes, and there's fruit and general farming over by Lake Michigan. Right through here the lumber industry is very important. And of course all the way up and onto the Upper Peninsula. On the higher land you'll find a maple, birch, elm, and basswood. Everything else is conifers. Do you like the woods?"

"I don't know," Link admitted. "I never spent enough time in them to find out."

"Well that's half the battle," Harriet said.

"Half the battle?"

"Of learning to like something different," she replied. "If you are willing to admit you don't know if you like something, you have a good chance. Most people are certain they won't like something that is unfamiliar. If you stopped and asked most of the men working at the lumber mills around here if they would like to go to a symphony concert in New York, they would say no. Actually they don't know because they have never been to one. I hope you'll like the woods."

"I like all this space, this wild country without people," Link said cautiously. He didn't add that he wasn't certain how long it would be before he got bored.

"It's too bad we can't see it the way it once was," Harriet said. "The whole Upper Peninsula and northern part of this area was once covered with the most magnificent stand of white pine, red pine, white spruce, white cedar, and hemlock in the world. Even the swamps had gigantic black spruce. The trees were two or three feet in diameter and towered eighty feet into the air. But they're gone now, like the passenger pigeon."

"What's a passenger pigeon?" Link asked. "I don't think I've ever seen one."

"I'm sure you haven't. They're extinct," Harriet said grimly. "I've never seen one either. I understand they were about the same shape and color as a mourning dove but were much larger and had long tails. Have you ever seen a mourning dove?"

"Once or twice," Link replied, trying to remember what the bird looked like. He did recall that it made a mourning cooing sound each morning and evening.

"Well, the passenger pigeon was once one of the most plentiful birds in America. It was all over the eastern part of the United States. Long after it became scarce in other parts, it used to nest in huge flocks in northern Michigan"—she paused a minute—"and was slaughtered by the thousands."

Oh, boy, Link thought. Aunt Harriet sounded like one of those conservation death-on-hunting nuts. His

Aunt Alice occasionally read something in the paper and gave everyone indignant lectures about how some animal was being exterminated. She made very little impression on Uncle Herbert.

"Look, Alice, I've never even seen one of these Santa Cruz long-toed salamanders you talk about," Uncle Herbert would say. "I'm not sure that I want to. I don't know exactly what I can do to make life better for it or if I should. Maybe it should become extinct. Maybe it just isn't fitted to survive in today's world."

Alice had sputtered and fumed and told Herbert that it was people like him that were ruining the environment.

"Well, I don't see what good it does to get all worked up and indignant in New York City when the poor lizard is in Santa Cruz," Herbert had replied. "Just what are *you* actually doing to help?"

"Why did they kill so many pigeons?" Link asked cautiously. After all, it was something to talk about.

"For food, supposedly," she replied. "But the slaughter was terribly wasteful—just as it was with the buffalo. The Indians around here for centuries used the pigeon as food. They went to the nesting areas and killed the squabs by the hundreds and smoked them for the fall and winter. There were so many pigeons and so few Indians that their hunting didn't matter. The white man was much more efficient. He killed pigeons by the millions. Your great-grandfather visited a nesting area when he was a boy, and it made a very great impression on him. When I was about eight he told me about it. His description was so vivid that I had nightmares for weeks."

"What did he say?" Link asked.

"The pigeons traveled in such huge flocks that they actually would blacken the sky. When they picked a nesting area they landed in such hordes that they broke limbs off trees and often killed smaller trees. I suppose they did a certain amount of crop and forest damage, but this is not the reason they were killed. They were delicious eating. Hunters made a business of killing them and shipping them to the city markets. Your great-grandfather had a number of Indian friends, and he went with the Indians to this nesting area."

"How long ago was that?" Link asked.

"About 1875," Harriet said. "That was the year of the great slaughter, I think. Over a million pigeons went to market from one nesting area alone. The market became glutted and pigeons were fed to the hogs."

Link looked around at the tree-covered land. It was fascinating to think that his great-grandfather had walked through these same woods a hundred years ago —and with Indian friends. Indians were something you saw on TV, the parts usually played by white men.

"What was so horrible about it?" he asked. "You said you had nightmares."

"I couldn't possibly repeat his description of the blood, the stench, and the slaughter. The Indians usually took only the fat squabs from the nests, but the white hunter used wholesale methods like lures of salt and grain. And worst of all he used a stool pigeon. Do you know what a stool pigeon is?"

"Someone who squeals on someone else," Link replied promptly.

"That's what it means now," Harriet said. "But a stool pigeon was a real pigeon that a hunter captured. He put its eyes out and fastened it to a perch or stool that could be raised or lowered to attract flocks that were flying low. The poor bird fluttered and attracted its mates. They came down, saw the grain and salt, and landed. The hunter pulled a net over them." Harriet Keller turned to look at her nephew. "The last passenger pigeon died in a zoo in Cleveland in 1914."

Harriet Keller's voice was somewhat nasal and high pitched, and she had a peculiar flat way of speaking. Link was used to the members of his family talking with great excitement, using their hands as they spoke, and showing how they felt by their facial expressions. Oddly, Harriet's matter-of-fact way of speaking made the story much more horrible. He felt much more concerned than he had after any of Aunt Alice's tirades.

"That's a terrible story," he said.

"Yes," Harriet agreed. "But there is nothing we can do about the passenger pigeon now. It wasn't my generation, let alone yours, that exterminated it. All we can do is make certain that we don't make similar mistakes."

"But aren't there laws protecting scarce animals and birds?" Link asked.

"Yes, but laws are only a small part of it. I used to think dwindling species were all the fault of the hunter. While that may be true in a few cases, I doubt if it usually is. Even if no one had ever killed a passenger pigeon, it probably would have become quite scarce. There were only a few million Indians on the North American continent when the white men came. Now there are two hundred million people, and the wilderness has given way to farms. Swamps have been drained, forests cut down, and houses and cities built. There just aren't the conditions or the room for the wild animals and birds that once lived here. It was inevitable that the huge herds of buffalo that roamed the plains had to go and be replaced by cattle. Any intelligent conservationist is aware of this."

"What's the answer?" Link asked.

"No one has the final answer," Harriet said. "I suppose some species will become extinct just as the dinosaurs did when the world conditions became wrong for them. However, there should be room enough and enough of the right habitat for all to have a chance of survival. And we don't know yet how important each bird, animal, fish, or insect is in the circle of life on this planet. The farmer kills a crow because it eats the corn he has just planted. He is making a mistake in my opinion. The crow will eat so many grasshoppers, beetles, and grubs that he will do more good than bad."

"It sounds complicated," Link said.

"It is complicated," Harriet said. "To me the conditions that our wildlife needs are the same conditions I find I need for happiness. I love the Upper Peninsula— I feel at peace there. The birds and animals still feel at home. And man, who gets nervous and exhausted from the problems of the city, needs the wilderness to restore his soul. In a way I'm opposed to some forms of progress. I'm sorry they built this bridge we're coming to."

Harriet might not show much emotion in her face and speech, but she felt strongly about certain things, Link decided. He was relieved in a way. It made her seem less cold and reserved to know that she got excited and upset even if she kept it bottled up. She would take some getting used to, however. He looked ahead and saw a long, long bridge stretching out ahead. The other end was so far away that it was out of sight.

"Quite a bridge," Link said.

"It's one of the longest in the world," Harriet Keller said. "The suspension arch is the third longest after the Verrazano and the Golden Gate bridges. But I would be willing to let someone else have all the honors and go across by ferry the way we used to do. I suppose it's convenient for those living on the Upper Peninsula, but it's going to bring tourists by the droves. Saint Ignace at the far end of this bridge used to be a nice quiet little town. Now it's a bustling city. We'll stop and get some fresh milk and a few things because it's the last good-sized town we'll come to before the cabin."

After they were across the bridge they turned off the highway into the business district of Saint Ignace. Lincoln felt his heart sink. If this was his aunt called a "bustling city," he couldn't imagine what the rest of the Upper Peninsula must be like. Saint Ignace was just a wide spot in the road as far as he was concerned. They bought some groceries, a pair of ankle-high boots, and two long-sleeved shirts for Link. Although it was not quite eleven o'clock, they were both hungry. They had a sandwich and continued on their way.

The road wound along the shore of Lake Michigan, first skirting the sand dunes and then climbing up into the heavily wooded hills. It was a beautiful drive for about forty miles, and the view out across the water and the sight of the sandy beaches made Link homesick for the Atlantic.

"Any surfing on Lake Michigan?" he asked hopefully.

"I'm afraid not," Harriet said. "The lake certainly gets rough enough, but there's no real surf of the kind you want."

Link sighed. Oh well, he didn't have a surfboard anyhow. Suddenly the road left the lake shore and plunged into the trees. The countryside grew increasingly wild and lonely. They went about twenty miles without meeting a car and then turned northward. The countryside grew even lonelier. They passed through mile after mile of forest, broken only by an occasional swamp, which was even more forbidding than the thick trees and underbrush.

"Doesn't anyone live here?" Link asked.

"Not many," Harriet Keller said happily. "The Seney Wildlife Refuge is to our left, and it's about a hundred thousand acres. There's a town just ahead, called Germfask. It's where we'll do most of our marketing."

Several miles later they passed through a tiny village. It consisted of a few houses, several stores and service stations, and a small stone church that seemed to have been constructed of huge round pebbles.

"Getting to be quite a town," Harriet said. "I suppose it's all the tourists visiting the wildlife refuge. They have paths you can walk and things like that."

"This is the nearest town?" Link asked in disbelief.

"That's right," Harriet replied. "Fortunately we aren't too near. About five miles."

Five miles to this little backwater, Link thought to himself. He saw exactly two people on the way through. Both were elderly men. Probably anyone under twenty was hiding in the bushes, he decided, afraid of strangers.

They went down a side road for about four miles. It was little more than a gravel track in the wilderness. Then Harriet spotted a black opening in the trees and turned down a narrow, winding trail. The trees and vines brushed against the windows of the car, and the station wagon jounced up and down over the bumpy ground. Twice they drove through shallow pools of water. Finally they came into a small clearing in the middle of which stood a weatherbeaten log cabin.

"This is it!" Harriet announced. "Isn't this lovely?"

She stopped the car near the front door. Link got out slowly and looked around. There was no doubting the excitement in Harriet Keller's voice. She thought the place was beautiful! Link looked around, trying to understand. The clearing in the wilderness was small, and what there was of it was carpeted with pine needles almost to the door. The tiny cabin was dwarfed by the towering pines and cedars. While the sun was shining brightly, gloom seemed to descend a few feet back in the forest. He could see into the trees only a short distance, and that looked dark and forbidding. Everywhere there was quiet. Link had never known anything like it. There were a few distant calls of birds and some strange half-whisperings of leaves as something moved in the underbrush. Otherwise the silence was complete. It was another world and Link did not feel at home in it. There were no sounds of automobiles, no voices, not even the hum of a distant plane. It was disturbing.

Harriet Keller walked slowly from her side of the car toward the trees, so intent she hardly used her cane. She looked around happily, inhaling the pine-scented air. For the moment she paid no attention to Link or anything else while she drank in the peace of the woods. Link glanced at her and saw that her thoughts were far away. He walked slowly around the cabin, glancing up now and then. There were no wires running to the cabin from anywhere. That meant no telephone or electric light. He supposed that little half-tumbled-down shack in back was what they called a privy or outhouse. A short distance away he saw a rusty iron pump. The drinking water evidently came from a well. What did you do if you wanted to take a bath? Pump a pail of water and pour it over your head?

He made a complete circuit of the cabin. Harriet Keller had walked a short distance into the trees and was looking upward. So this was the cabin he had heard about! A log hut in the middle of a wilderness, miles from civilization. No electric light, no television, not even a refrigerator. What in the world could you do in a place like this? Talk to the birds? He couldn't imagine spending an entire summer in what could only be called an uncomfortable shack. He'd go crazy with boredom.

"Well, what do you think?" Harriet asked, coming back toward the car. "It's a beautiful spot isn't it?"

Link was tempted to say no, it was not a beautiful spot and that he was ready to head back for New Jersey. He'd seen enough of the Upper Peninsula. But he didn't.

"It's quiet and peaceful," he said. "I guess I better unload the car."

3

The cabin had only three rooms. Most of the space was taken up by one large room that served as the kitchen, dining, and living area. An old-fashioned kitchen range stood near one corner, and a big stone fireplace occupied the middle of the opposite wall. There was a cedar plank table, four straight chairs, several easy chairs that looked worn but comfortable, some built-in cupboards, and a worktable near the stove. Two doors led to the two smaller rooms. Each contained a bed, with what appeared to be a new mattress, a straight chair, an old bureau, and a small closet.

The floors were of worn planks, and the inside of the log walls had been paneled with boards. Inside, the cabin was much cozier and inviting than Link had expected. It was clean and had none of the musty smell that houses usually have after being closed for a long time.

"Charley and his wife did a good job cleaning the

place," Harriet said approvingly. "He has looked after the cabin for years—kept the roof tight, repaired the windows, things like that. When I wrote him that I was coming up this summer, he said that the squirrels and mice had got in and had ruined the mattresses. So I sent up two new ones. He's put new screens on the windows, and I noticed before we came in that he'd set out some tomato plants for us. He's a wonderful man. You'll like him."

"What is Charley's last name?" Link asked.

"Horse."

"You're not serious?"

"His real name is Running Horse," Harriet said. He's a Chippewa Indian. He used to work in the lumber camps as a young man, and someone called him Charley Horse and he's kept the name ever since. He knows more about the woods than anyone I've ever known. He's an expert guide."

Link unloaded the station wagon while his aunt put things away. Then he went to the pile of wood that Charley Horse had left near the edge of the clearing and brought in wood for the kitchen stove.

"We used to have an outdoor fireplace," Harriet said. "It was built of stones stacked together. If we can find the metal grill, we can rebuild it. Then we can cook out of doors part of the time. In the middle of the summer it's too hot to build a fire in the stove. We usually didn't unless it rained."

"What about a refrigerator?" Link asked, looking at

the cases of Coca-Cola and ginger ale he had carried in from the car.

"I've talked about getting one of those gas refrigerators for years," Harriet said. "But I just haven't bothered. There's a spring not very far away. We used to use it for our drinking water when your father and I were children. Later we drilled a well. But I still use the spring to keep things cold, like butter. We put whatever we want in one of those metal pails and put the pail in the water. As for the bottles of soda, just tie a string around the necks and lower them into the water. You'll be surprised how cold they'll get."

They had lamb chops, canned peas, and baking powder biscuits for dinner. Then Harriet got her cane, and with Link carrying the large metal pail full of perishables they walked through the gathering gloom down an overgrown path to the spring. It was not far. The trail sloped downward for a short distance and then wound around a small hillock. Water gushed out of a low ledge of rock and trickled down into a pool about ten feet in diameter. A tiny stream led the overflow away into the darkness of the woods.

"I think the water is perfectly safe to drink," Harriet said. "The real reason Dad had the well put in was that he and your father liked to come down here to take baths. Mother objected to that. She said she wasn't going to drink bath water even if it was running."

Link leaned over and put his hand in the water. "It's ice cold," he said.

"Much too cold to bathe in, I always thought," she agreed. "Mother and I carried water and took a bath with warm water in a tub."

Link found a flat rock ledge in the pool, placed the pail on it, and then weighted it down with another rock."

"That will do fine unless some bear gets too inquisitive," Harriet said. "One year I had real trouble. Charley put a rope up over that limb, and I suspended the pail out in the middle of the pool. I had to use a long stick with a hook on the end to reach out and get it."

"Are there many bears around here?" Lincoln asked, looking back into the thick depths of the woods.

"Lots of them. But if you leave them alone, they'll usually leave you alone."

It was dark by the time they returned to the cabin. Harriet lighted a kerosene lamp and showed Link how it worked. "I imagine you're tired," she said. "Up here you'll find you just naturally get up with the light and go to bed with the dark."

Link went outside and brushed his teeth at the pump and then went to bed. When he blew out the lamp, complete darkness descended. There were no distant street lights outside his window and no occasional flash of headlights. The room was so totally black that it bothered him. He glanced at his watch just to be certain that nothing had happened to his eyes. After about ten minutes he was able to make out the square of his window, a slightly grayer shade of black in the black wall.

Suddenly he heard something rustling around outside. It sounded enormous. Charley Horse had put new screens on the windows, but would a screen discourage a bear? He tried to convince himself that if iron bars had been needed, they would have been put on. The rustling was suddenly replaced by a gnawing sound as though a rat the size of a bear were gnawing down a big tree. There were lots of trees, he decided, one more or less would make no difference as long as it didn't fall on him. He had just become resigned to the gnawing, when suddenly the night was pierced with a blood-chilling screech: "*Oouuooouuuoo, oh oh oh!*" This brought him bolt upright in bed. Then he lay back down again. He'd read of screech owls. The screech was repeated, and then in the distance he heard a high-pitched barking, like a dog but still not a dog. The peace and quiet of the deep woods! he thought disgustedly. What he needed was a few trucks or cement mixers driving down the street so he could get to sleep. He covered his ears with his pillow and closed his eyes.

He drifted off to sleep in spite of the strange noises, and the next thing he knew it was light and he was awake. He could smell coffee. He got dressed, went out to the pump, and sloshed cold water over his face. On his way back he noticed the broom that had been left beside the door. It had fallen to the ground, and something had gnawed the handle half through. He carried it inside and held it up for Harriet to see.

"Porcupine," she said with a laugh. "I think it's the salt in the perspiration from your hands that they're after. They'll sometimes gnaw a hoe handle in two in a night. Did you hear that owl screeching last night?"

"I heard lots of animals, and I see signs of them, but I don't see them," Link objected.

"Once in a while you will just stumble onto an animal, but usually they are very wary and cautious. So you have to be even more wary and quiet. If you stand quietly any place long enough, you'll be surprised at what you'll see."

While they ate breakfast, Harriet drew a rough map of the surrounding area, pointing out what she thought might interest him.

"It's always a good idea to carry a compass if you go very far into the woods," she cautioned. "It's not so much that a compass will keep you from getting lost, but if you do get lost, you can then keep going in one direction. Eventually, even up here, you will come to a road."

She produced a small compass, which Link stuck in his pocket before he went exploring. He found the swamp that Harriet had indicated, and the sizable stream of dark brown water that led away from it through the trees to the Manistique River. He located the old beaver dam and a pond above it. And he visited the remains of what Harriet had said was an old stagecoach station. They were interesting, he admitted, but you couldn't stand around for hours and look at a beaver dam or a tumble-down log cabin. By the middle of the afternoon he had seen practically everything on Harriet's crude map. He was on his way back to the cabin when he passed by the spring. Walking through the woods was much warmer work than he had expected, and the water looked inviting. He stripped off his clothes and stepped into the edge of the pool.

The water was icy. It was so cold that his feet felt numb in a matter of seconds. He looked out at the center of the pool. The water was at least four feet deep. His father used to take a bath here, he told himself. He could at least take a quick dip. Holding his breath, he made a shallow dive toward the center. The water was deeper than he had expected; when he stood up it came to his chin. He had never been so cold in his life. With his teeth chattering he waded as quickly as possible to the edge and climbed out.

He found a spot of sunshine and stood shivering in it for several minutes while he tried to brush off some of the water from his body. He was covered with goose pimples. He put on his clothes and then sat down by the pool for a while. He felt wonderful. That quick dip had been the most fun of anything since his arrival in Michigan. But that was only a minute. What was he going to do with an entire summer?

The next day he went into Germfask with his aunt to buy some milk and a few other staples. They visited the

Seney Wildlife Refuge Headquarters, looked at the exhibits, and Link watched some Canada geese on the pond just outside the main building. When they returned to the cabin he wrote several letters and took several short aimless walks into the woods. The following morning he weeded the area around the tomato plants and then thumbed aimlessly through one of his aunt's bird books.

"You're bored, aren't you?" Harriet asked in the middle of lunch.

The sudden question caught Link unprepared. "Well, I don't know what you find to do all summer up here," he admitted finally. "What did my dad do when he was a boy?"

"He was like me. He could lie hidden in the underbrush and watch a beaver or a heron all day long. You have to love the creatures of the wild to like it here I guess. I find New York City terribly dull." She reached out a hand and touched him on the arm. "I suppose in a way the whole idea of coming up here was selfish. Now that I am partially crippled I don't feel up to staying here alone the way I once did. So I told myself that you would enjoy it so that I could come. I love it here. I can hobble outside and just sit watching and have a wonderful time. And of course there *was* the chance that you might like it too. Would you like to leave?"

"Well, I haven't really given it a trial yet," Link said, reluctant to hurt her by saying that he would.

"You've run out of things to do," Harriet observed. "I suppose you ought to try to get that picture your uncle wanted before you leave."

"Yes, I'd forgotten that," Link agreed. "Where would I go to find sandhill cranes?"

"Lakes, marshes, wet areas," Harriet said. "There are a number of these around within a few miles. Why don't we leave it that you will stay long enough to get your pictures. Then we'll pack up and leave."

"That's fair enough," Link said, feeling much better.

"I want to go pay Charley Horse for his work here and see several other people," Harriet said, getting up from the table. "You don't mind being left here alone?"

"Not at all," Link said.

He went to his room, got out his Uncle Albert's camera, and picked a 105 mm. lens. There were only four exposures left on the roll of film, so he went outside and used them up taking pictures of the cabin. Then he reloaded the camera, tucked his aunt's bird guide in his pocket, and started off through the woods. There might be a sandhill crane at the old beaver pond. "Wet areas," Harriet had said. He might be lucky and get his pictures right away. If he did, he wouldn't say anything but wait until he got the developed slides back. He could put up with another week or so buried in the woods. Then Harriet wouldn't feel she had completely wasted her money having the cabin repaired.

He spent the next hour crouched beside the pond,

trying to sit quietly, but it was almost impossible. Tiny insects buzzed around his face, crawled down his collar, and generally made him miserable. At first he tried to swat them but decided this was a waste of time. Finally he crawled underneath a low shrub and, with the leaves almost brushing his face, managed to find a little peace.

He waited as patiently as he knew how, but he saw nothing that either resembled a crane or a crane's nest. According to his bird book they didn't build much of a nest—just a shallow cluster of sedge grass and twigs on the ground. The trouble was that the edges of the pond were thick with sedges, reeds, and cattails, and it would have been difficult to see a standing crane, much less a nest. He was about to give up and move on, when suddenly, almost in front of him in the middle of the pond there was a floating bird. It looked slightly like a small duck with a long, slender neck. Its back was gray-brown and it had a white bill. Link raised his camera to his eyes and looked through the telescopic lens. There was a black band around the whitish bill. He snapped pictures and then put his camera down gently. He began thumbing through the book trying to find a picture of the floating bird. He made a slight sound as he turned the pages and when he looked up the bird was slowly sinking into the water. It sank lower and lower until finally just its eyes were above the water. He watched fascinated as it disappeared entirely. He waited and waited until he decided that something must have pulled it under and eaten it. Then suddenly it popped to the surface about twenty feet farther away. Link watched as the bird dived several times. It could disappear in a flash or sink slowly and then reappear fifteen or twenty feet away. He wished that he could swim like that underwater. Finally it disappeared for a much longer period of time. His eyes searched the surface of the pond looking for it. Then, entirely by chance, he saw its head slowly emerging in the reeds, not very far from where he sat. It came up slowly, its neck turning cautiously like a submarine periscope. Suddenly it hopped onto what seemed to be a floating pile of reeds. It scratched away some covering reeds and sat down on a nest.

Slowly and cautiously, Link raised his camera and took several pictures. He had been sitting within a few yards of the nest for some time without seeing it. He understood now what Harriet had meant when she said if he sat still long enough he would see things.

After ten minutes of thumbing through his book, he decided that the strange bird that could impersonate a submarine was a pied-bill grebe. He sat quietly for another hour. He saw blue jays and several songbirds that he could not identify and then—for a few hopeful minutes—he thought he saw a sandhill crane. An enormous bird flew high overhead on slow, flapping wings. Link looked at it through his camera lens. It was blue-gray, but it had no red crown on its head. His Uncle

Albert had warned him not to confuse the great blue heron with the sandhill crane.

"A crane flies with his neck stretched out straight and a heron curves his in an S curve," Albert had said.

He was growing stiff and restless, and buzzing insects continued to plague him, so he decided to call it a day, go back, and have a quick dip in the spring. He took a slightly different route and passed through a small natural clearing that he had not visited before. He was partway across when he realized that several birds, including a particularly noisy blue jay, were screaming excitedly about something. He stopped and looked around carefully, searching for the cause of all the fuss. He looked first at the ground and then at the lower branches of the trees. Suddenly he saw an animal about eighteen inches long up in a maple tree at the edge of the clearing. Whether it was the cause of the birds' alarm or not he had no idea, but it was so grotesque-looking that he forgot about the birds. He raised his camera to use the lens as his binoculars. The animal had sort of yellowish tinged hair and a back and tail covered with white spikes. It was a porcupine! It seemed to be staring straight at him.

He moved slowly toward the tree. The porcupine made no move to run away or even to hide behind the tree trunk.

That would make quite a picture, he thought, as he watched the animal with its ratlike face and eyes. The

trouble was that a branch partially blocked his view. He circled trying to get a clear shot. Either maple leaves or the feathery branches of a nearby spruce kept him from getting a good picture. The porcupine still showed no sign of being afraid.

He looked at a low branch thoughtfully. If he climbed up about level with the animal he could get a beautiful shot. There would be nothing in the way, and he could take the picture from the correct angle as far as the light was concerned. What a story that would make when he got back home! "I was in the same tree as the porcupine when I took this shot," he would say casually.

He slung the camera over his shoulder so that it hung against his back. Then he reached up, grabbed the lowest limb, and began climbing. It was not difficult but he went slowly and cautiously, keeping a wary eye on the porcupine. He got up about ten feet, just slightly below the porcupine, propped himself in a reasonably secure position, and got his camera. He took several shots and then moved a trifle closer. The porcupine began to show the first signs of nervousness. It retreated along its branch, moving about three feet farther out. The fact that it seemed frightened of him gave Link more courage. He climbed one branch higher and leaned over to get at just the right angle. He snapped one picture and then leaned farther to the left. He was too intent on getting the picture, and his right foot slipped. He began to topple. He grabbed frantically for the nearest branch—

which was the one on which the porcupine was perched. He caught it. The sudden weight on the small branch shook the porcupine off. Link was too busy to notice or care what happened to the porcupine. His right foot slipped off the branch completely, throwing most of his weight on his left foot. The branch on which it was resting was small, and it snapped. That left him with only his right hand grasping one branch. His left hand still held the precious camera. The branch was too big around to hold properly, and it was doubtful if he could have held himself by one hand anyway. He did manage to hold on long enough to allow his feet to swing over so that he was dangling upright. Then he let go and dropped.

It was not a long drop, and he landed on his feet on soft ground. Slightly off balance, he stumbled backward and sat down heavily. There was an instant searing pain. He let out a yelp of agony and dropped the camera. It fell only a few inches to the ground which was carpeted with leaves and pine needles. Link was not much interested whether the camera was safe or not. He was in too much agony. He felt as though he were sitting on a red-hot stove. He rolled over until he was on his hands and knees. Then he reached back and felt the seat of his pants with his hand, half expecting to feel blood. Instead he felt what seemed to be stiff needles. He looked around suddenly for the porcupine. It was gone, but it had left plenty to remember it by. The entire seat of his pants was filled with quills! He had either landed on or beside the porcupine when he sat down.

Slowly and gingerly he got to his feet. Each movement was painful. He reached around and carefully took hold of the nearest quill he could see. He gave a yank. Nothing happened except he felt a sharp pain in his behind.

He picked up the camera and slowly started toward the cabin. Each step was torture. He paused every few feet, but he couldn't sit down. There was nothing to do but to plod onward, trying to move with the least amount of pain. About two thirds of the way he leaned against a tree, sort of half lying on his stomach, and examined the camera. It seemed unharmed. He blew away a few specks of dirt on the lens and got the lens cap from his pocket and put it on. At least he had got some good shots before he fell. And what a story he would have to tell now when he showed the family those slides!

He reached the cabin, went to his room, and lay face down on his bed. Once more he tried pulling a quill. He had no more success than before. Those things were in there to stay! He could see himself being wheeled into a hospital, face down on the stretcher. The doctor would operate while the nurses and everyone stood around laughing.

He was wondering how he would ever get to the hospital when he heard his aunt drive in. He waited until she had entered the cabin.

"Would you come in here, Aunt Harriet?" he called. "I had an accident!"

Harriet came into the room. Link turned to look at her. She glanced at him without changing her expression and said, "Yes, you certainly did. And I'll bet it's painful! What did you do, sit on him?"

"I guess," he said. "I climbed a tree to take his picture and we both fell."

"Hurt yourself otherwise?" she asked.

"Nope. It was rough walking home though."

"I'll bet it was," she said. "Well, we have to get those quills out. Each quill is covered with dozens of little barbs. That makes them hard to pull out. But if you don't pull them out they work deeper. You can't possibly take off your pants. I'll have to pull the quills out through the cloth. The best way is to take a pair of pliers and give a quick yank. I've got some antiseptic that has sort of a chilling effect, and I'll try to spray you thoroughly with that. Maybe it will soak through your trousers and deaden the pain a little. But I warn you it will hurt."

"Go ahead," Link said, relieved that he wouldn't have to go to the hospital.

Harriet left and returned a few minutes later with a pair of pliers from the car and a can of antiseptic spray. She sprayed Link's posterior thoroughly and then asked, "Ready?"

"I guess as ready as I'll ever be," Link said. He pressed his lips together.

66

There was a sudden stab of pain, and Harriet said, "That's one! There's quite a few to go!"

"Don't count them," Link said. "I don't want to know how many until it's all over."

"The Indians dyed porcupine quills and used them to decorate deerskin shirts and pouches and moccasins," she said some time later as she yanked out the fifteenth quill.

"I'm going to save these and use them to decorate a poster that says "Beware of Porcupines," Link said. He clenched his teeth as she gave another yank.

She pulled out twenty-two quills altogether. Link was sore and he knew he would be unable to sit comfortably for several days, but at least he could walk without pain.

"You'd better take off your clothes and examine yourself closely to be certain we haven't missed any. And then spray yourself with disinfectant again."

Link followed her suggestion and then dressed. "I'm going down to the spring," he announced as he walked into the main room of the cabin. "The other day when I waded in, my feet were numb by the time I'd gone three feet. Maybe if I sit down for fifteen minutes I can get the same results."

Harriet gave a slight chuckle. "I don't blame you." He had reached the door when she said, "Link."

He turned.

"I want you to know that I realize how painful that was," she said, almost shyly. "Not even the 'stoic redskin,' as they say, could have complained less."

She was much more sympathetic than he had thought, he decided, as he went on toward the spring. But she didn't know how to express it. He was beginning to understand her a little, and the more he understood her the better he liked her. She was really quite a good egg.

4

Link spent most of the following two days lying on his stomach in bed. He was annoyed that he hadn't brought something along to read like a good science-fiction book. However, he had brought a pad of paper so he spent an hour making a sketch of a porcupine. Harriet, who came in to see if he wanted anything, looked at his efforts critically for a moment.

"Very good," she said finally. "I didn't realize you could draw like that. You should give him more prominent teeth. He has two upper and two lower incisors that are almost like chisels. He uses these to rip off the outer layer of bark to get at the tender inner layers. I don't know why, but his teeth are orange."

"I'm not sure about his tail either," Link said, looking at his sketch. "I think maybe it ought to be a little broader."

"I think I have a picture," Harriet said. She left the room and returned with two books on wild animals and several more on birds. "That one on the animals of Michigan has some good photos in it," she said.

Link began thumbing through the books and spent most of the remainder of the day reading. The details of wild-animal habits were surprisingly interesting. Beavers in particular fascinated him. He read that one beaver in a single night could gnaw down an aspen six inches in diameter, cut it into six-foot lengths, and haul the logs some distance to his pond. While he was hunting for a sandhill crane, he would keep an eye out for an active beaver colony.

The third day after his meeting with the porcupine he felt more like moving around. He even ate his lunch sitting down, although he used a pillow. During the middle of the afternoon he walked down to the spring for a quick dip. He felt much better and decided that the following day he would set out again to find a sandhill crane. Harriet had found a detailed map of the area. He would try some bigger lake or pond.

There was a battered ex-army Jeep sitting in front of the cabin when he returned from the spring. Harriet was inside having a cup of coffee with an ancient-looking man in khaki trousers and a faded blue shirt. One sleeve had been cut off the shirt and folded over because the wearer had no use for it: his left arm was missing.

His deeply tanned face looked as though it were made

of a piece of worn leather, and his short black hair was sprinkled with gray. There were countless seams and wrinkles around his eyes and the corners of his mouth, but his dark, deep-set eyes were keen and he wore no glasses.

"Charley, I want you to meet my nephew Lincoln," Harriet said. "Link this is Charley Horse."

They shook hands. Charley's hand was hard and his grip made Link wince.

"You look something like your father did when he was your age," Charley said. Charley's perfectly normal speech for some reason surprised Link. He had half expected to hear the grunts that were the movie version of an Indian's attempts at English.

"Yes, he does," Harriet agreed. "Especially around the eyes."

"How do you like the woods?" Charley asked.

"Fine," Link said, deciding to give a polite answer even if it wasn't exactly the truth. "Better than the porcupines seem to like me."

Charley grinned. "It's wise to stay at least ten feet away from a porky. They can't throw their quills, but they can swing that tail back and forth and a quill can come loose and fly several feet."

"Link wants to get some color pictures of a sandhill crane," Harriet said. "Do you know where any are nesting this year?"

"I haven't noticed any this year but then I haven't

been looking," Charley replied. "Pocket Marsh used to have a few. It's the nearest spot, I guess."

"I've looked at the old Beaver Pond near here," Link told him.

Charley shook his head. "Too small. Sandhill cranes like big marshes—fifty or a hundred acres at least. I could show you the way to Pocket Marsh tomorrow morning if you'd like."

"That would be fine," Link said.

Charley got up to leave, and they all walked outside. The Indian looked around and gave a low whistle. A few seconds later a nondescript dog appeared and sat down beside Charley's heels. The dog was about the size of an airedale and looked as though it might be part airedale and possibly part collie, German shepherd, and English setter. Link decided that was enough when the dog went to investigate a nearby bug. Link watched it trotting the few feet. Its body seemed unusually long for its legs, so Link threw in a dachshund ancestor too. Whatever the dog was, it was certainly a mixed-up mess as far as looks went.

"What kind of dog is he?" Link asked.

"Very smart dog," Charley said proudly.

"I mean what breed of dog is he?" Link asked.

Charley shrugged expressively. "Who knows?" He looked at Link and grinned. "Like the white man, a mixture."

Charley got in the car, and the dog, in spite of his

short legs, managed to jump in the rear, and they went clattering off through the woods.

"He's shifting gears," Link said, listening to the Jeep. "How's he do it with only one hand?"

"He can do most anything with one arm that other people do with two," Harriet said. "He has some sort of attachment on the gearshift, and he shifts with his right knee."

"What happened to his arm?" Link asked.

"I don't know," Harriet said. "I haven't wanted to ask, and he has never volunteered the information."

Link returned to the cabin and sat down on his pillow to write some letters. He wrote a short note to his mother, telling her of his brush with the porcupine. He thought about telling her that he expected to leave shortly but decided to wait until he could give her a definite date. Then he wrote Pedro, with whom he felt free to say exactly what he thought of Michigan's north woods.

DEAR PEDRO,

I'm really out in the wilds. This is about as lonely a spot as I ever hope to find. We have no electricity, no running water, no inside toilet, and only a wood stove to cook with. We go to bed when it gets dark but not to sleep. I know what they mean when they talk about a howling wilderness—this is it! There are raccoons, opossums, deer, wolves, bear, fox, martens, and porcupines according to a book I'm reading. All of them gather outside my window at night and kill each other. All I've seen so far is a porcupine. I not only saw him, I fell out of a tree on him. My aunt had to pull twenty-two quills out of my behind. I hope I don't run into a moose!

There's not much to do around here, and as soon as I snap a picture of one of those goofy sandhill cranes I'm heading back toward civilization. My aunt says this is a bird paradise and she's right. There are fifty million little gnats buzzing around your face wherever you go. That's one good reason why there are so few people. As far as I'm concerned the place belongs to the birds. What I wouldn't give for a good ice-cream soda and someone to talk to. I don't think there's anyone my age within twenty miles. Except for the woods full of animals there's just me, my half-crippled old maid aunt, and a one-armed Indian. And that's one person too many—me!

REGARDS,
Link

To Link's surprise, his aunt awakened him shortly after five the next morning.

"What's wrong?" he asked sleepily.

"Nothing," she replied. "But I know Charley. When he says morning he means exactly that—when the sun comes up. Breakfast is almost ready."

Link had not finished his bacon and eggs when he heard Charley's Jeep clatter into the yard. He gulped down the last of his breakfast and went to his room for

74

his camera and some film. When he returned his aunt handed him a knapsack. "There're sandwiches in it. Two are for you and two are for Charley. Some days he goes all day without food so he may not eat his sandwiches himself. He may feed them to his dog so don't be surprised. He treats that dog like a person. Also there's some insect repellent in there. You'll need it to be able to sit beside the marsh in comfort."

Link went outside and joined Charley and his dog. The Indian had climbed out of his Jeep and was sitting quietly on a log, gazing into the trees.

"Just saw a raccoon over there" he said. He got to his feet. "There's no way to drive very close to the marsh, so we might as well leave on foot from here. Besides you'll want to know the way from here so you'll be able to go back by yourself in case we find cranes."

They set off through the trees. Link soon discovered that a day in the woods with Charley Horse was an experience unlike any he had ever known. Inside of ten minutes Link was completely lost. Charley seemed to wander aimlessly through the woods, going in no particular direction. As Link was to learn later, the old Indian knew the terrain so well that he chose the easiest routes even though they were often indirect. He skirted bogs that Link did not see, avoided thickets that were difficult to push through, and detoured to reach the easiest spot to ford a stream. While he was threading his way through the woods with such certainty, his eyes seemed to be everywhere except on where he was going. His sharp gaze wandered from the treetops to the underbrush and missed nothing. He pointed out a bald eagle's nest in a treetop, a skunk that stared curiously at them from beneath a protecting shrub, and a spruce grouse that stood so motionless and blended so perfectly with its surroundings that Charley had to point it out twice before Link managed to spot it.

Charley slipped through the woods effortlessly and quietly. He seemed to know instinctively where the ground was soft, when a log was too rotten to bear his weight, and when a rock would teeter if stepped on when crossing a stream. He brushed past briers that reached out to snag Link. Charley was over seventy, Harriet had said. Here Link was, about one fifth the Indian's age, and he was having trouble keeping up with him and even more trouble seeing what was going on in the woods around them. It was hot and humid, and he gave a sigh of relief when Charley sat down to rest beside a small stream after about an hour's travel.

"It's all right to drink," the Indian said, nodding toward the water. "We'll wait for Dog. He charged off after a raccoon, I think, and is quite a way behind."

Charley didn't explain how he knew the dog was far behind, and Link was too tired to wonder at the moment. He leaned over the stream, cupped his hands, and drank some water. It was delicious.

"Which way is the cabin?" he asked. "I'm all mixed up."

"That way," Charley replied promptly, pointing to the southwest. "Pocket Marsh is that way." He swung his arm around to the northeast. He looked at Link's puzzled face and picked up a stick.

"We came this way," he explained, drawing a winding zigzag on the ground. He pointed. "Swampy ground there so we went around. That ground was cut over a few years back and is full of bushes and briers. So we went around that. I'll draw you a map when we get back to the cabin."

They sat for another five minutes, and then Charley got to his feet.

"Here he comes," he announced. "Now we'll go."

Link had not heard a sound, but a minute later the dog appeared beside them. He looked hot, dirty, and out of breath.

"What's his name?" he asked Charley.

"Dog," the Indian replied.

They went through the woods for at least another mile. The character of the woods changed from pines, spruce, and balsams to maple and beech and other hardwoods. Charley paused by a small beech and pointed at some scars on the trunk well over Link's head. "Black bear," he said. "He's scratched the bark with his claws."

"Why?"

"No one is certain," Charley replied. "Some people say it's to mark his territory. Others to clean and sharpen his claws. On some beech trees they claw the tree to get up in it and eat the beechnuts. Other trees they just seem to claw because they like to. But no matter what the reason, when you see fresh scratches it means the bear has been around recently."

"Are black bears dangerous?" Link asked.

"They can be," Charley said. "Usually they will run away from a man, but don't try to get too close to one. So many tourists think it's fun to feed bears that a bear may get tame and expect food from everyone. Then if he doesn't get it, he gets mad."

After what seemed hours of walking, they finally approached the edge of the marsh. Link glanced at his watch. It was not yet nine o'clock. Putting his finger to his lips for silence, Charley carefully skirted the marsh, staying well back in the trees until they reached a slight hummock.

"We can go right up beside the water here and find a dry place to sit down. We must be very quiet and very patient."

Dog seemed to sense the need for stealth because he crept quietly along beside Charley. They reached the edge of the marsh and sat down beneath a sheltering shrub. Charley pointed out at the huge expanse of reeds and sedge grass that stretched out in front of them for at least half a mile.

"Sandhill cranes like this kind of country," he whispered. "Now we sit, we watch, and we wait."

And that was exactly what they did for the next two hours. Charley sat quietly, scarcely moving a muscle, staring out over the water. He was so quiet that several times Link wondered if he were asleep. However, each time he turned to look at Charley's face, he found that he was wide awake. Shortly after eleven, Charley got to his feet and quietly led Link back into the woods until they came to a small stream. He lay down beside it and drank.

"By this time of year young cranes are big enough to leave the nest and feed with the old birds but not old enough to fly," Charley explained. "So the old birds lead them out in open areas and along the edges of the marshes looking for food from daybreak until about this time of the morning. Then they roost some place until about the middle of the afternoon. There's not much chance of seeing them until they come out again. They feed until dark. We might as well move to a new spot."

They skirted along the edge of the marsh for half an hour or so, frequently making deep detours into the woods to avoid bogs. Finally about noon they reached another patch of high ground bordering the marsh. They sat down on a fallen tree, and Link got out his sandwiches and offered them to Charley. The old Indian took one, most of which he fed to his dog.

"Cranes like to build their nests in the water but near higher ground like this," he explained. "As soon as the young ones hatch, the old ones lead them over to a dry spot like this. If there's any danger the old ones give a warning and fly off. The young ones hide."

"It doesn't sound like the parents take very good care of the young," Link said.

"Yes, they do," Charley said. "The young ones can hide so that you never find them. I've only know one person who was able to capture one. That was by giving the call of the old ones—a sort of a *pur-r-r*."

"Who was that?" Link asked.

Charley held up a finger for silence and pointed out at the marsh. There in the shallow water several hundred yards away was a big bird. Link put his camera to his eye and looked through the telescopic lens. It was a striped brown bird with a long neck and long yellow legs. He was carefully wading in the shallow water, dipping his beak into the water now and then as he found something worth eating or investigating. Every few seconds he would pause to raise his head and look around warily.

"Thunder pumper," Charley said, leaning forward and whispering softly in Link's ear.

"Not a crane?" Link asked.

Charley shook his head. "He's a heron. Your aunt calls him a bittern. He has magic—he can disappear."

"What do you mean?" Link asked.

"Wait," Charley said. "He's coming closer."

They sat for another ten minutes while the bird waded in and out through the reeds, working his way gradually closer to where they sat.

"Watch him carefully," Charley warned. He picked

up a stick and tossed it out into the water, where it landed with a small splash. Link glanced for an instant at the stick, and when he looked back the bird was gone. It had not flown away because the air was empty. He raised his eyebrows at Charley and made motions with his hand to ask if it had dived. Charley grinned and shook his head.

"Look where he was and watch," he said. "And wait."

Link put the camera to his eye and looked through it at the spot where the bird had been. He steadied the camera on his knee and waited patiently for several minutes. Finally a faint motion caught his attention. And suddenly there was the bird again. He turned to Charley and nodded.

"Now keep your eyes on him all the time—not the stick," Charley warned.

As the Indian tossed a second stick into the water, Link kept his eye steadily on the bird. At the sound the bittern stretched its neck straight up and froze. The striped feathers of his body and neck merged with the brown stalks of last year's reeds. There was a slight breeze, and the bird seemed to sway with the cattails. Even through the camera lens it was difficult to distinguish him from the reeds.

"He's wonderful," Link said, fascinated. "A real camouflage expert."

They sat beside the marsh for another two hours and

a half. They saw squirrels, songbirds, another bittern, and a number of ducks but no sandhill cranes.

"No cranes today," Charley said finally. "If there is a roosting area some of the yearling birds might come in around dark but Miss Keller is expecting you back for dinner."

They started through the woods. Dog, who had disappeared about one o'clock, mysteriously appeared again and followed at Charley's heels. This time they seemed to be headed in a still different direction.

"There's a road over this way," Charley said. "From here it will be faster than the way we came."

They hiked about four miles through the woods and then suddenly came onto a blacktop road. They had gone a short distance along this when Dog set up a furious barking ahead and off to the right of the road. When they got opposite him, Charley left the road and plunged back into the trees to investigate. Link followed. A minute later they saw the cause of the commotion. A deer was lying in a thicket. It made no effort to get up although it was terrified. Charley circled around it several times, looking at it carefully.

"Broken leg," he said finally. "Probably hit by a car. It got this far but it won't get any farther. We'll have to shoot it." He turned to the dog. "Where's the fawn, Dog? Find the fawn. It's hiding some place near."

The dog understood what was wanted. Link and Charley began making widening circles.

"It has a spotted coat, and it will be very still," Charley warned. "Almost as hard to see as the thumper pumper."

Even after the warning, Link walked right by the hiding fawn. Dog discovered it a moment later. It was curled up beneath a small bush against the root of a tree, motionless and amost invisible. Charley made a quick grab and caught it. He produced some cord from his pocket and tied its legs.

"You stay here," he suggested. "I'll go get the Jeep and come back. "Miss Keller will have a gun."

"Aunt Harriet have a gun?" Link asked doubtfully.

"Sure," Charley replied. "Everyone in the woods has a gun and knows how to shoot. She's a good shot."

They left the wounded deer undisturbed but carried the fawn to the edge of the road. Link sat down gratefully and watched in amazement as Charley set off down the road at a flat-footed trot. After all the walking they had done that day, Link wouldn't have thought of trotting. Somehow Charley had managed to tell Dog that he was to wait or Dog was smart enough to figure it out. He sat down beside Link and went to sleep.

Forty-five minutes later, Link heard the sound of cars. Charley appeared in his Jeep, followed by Harriet in her station wagon. Charley disappeared into the woods and a minute later there was a sharp report. Then Charley came back and threw the carcass of the deer in the back of his Jeep.

"I'll go see the police," he said. "I'll tell them you have the fawn."

"Buy me a half dozen cans of milk," Harriet said, handing Charley some money. "I have a few on hand, so there's no rush to get them back to me."

"Do you have a baby bottle?" the Indian asked.

"I always have a baby bottle," Harriet replied. "Remember those two raccoons the last time I was up here?"

"Yes, they stole my pie," Charley said. He looked at Link. "I'll be by tomorrow."

He drove off down the road while they were loading the little fawn into the back of the car. It was frightened, but it made no effort to escape.

"You're going to feed it from a baby bottle?" Link asked.

"We'll try," Harriet said. "This one seems to be quite young and will probably take milk. It was probably that doe's first fawn. After the first fawn they usually have twins."

"What would happen if you didn't feed it?" Link asked.

"It would die," Harriet said. "It's pretty much dependent on its mother's milk yet. It needs its mother for protection almost as much as for the milk."

Link looked back at the tiny spotted creature. It was not enjoying the ride, and its big liquid eyes looked up at him in bewildered appeal. "Will it get tame?" he asked.

"Too tame," Harriet said. "Then it won't be prepared to go back to the woods and fend for itself. Or it will walk up to some hunter and get shot."

"How long will you have to feed it?"

"Fawns are usually weaned by the end of August or early September," Harriet said. "But since we won't be up here that long, we'll just take care of it until we can find someone to take it off our hands."

They returned to the cabin, and Link made a small pen in one corner of the big room using several boxes and two boards that he found. He carried the fawn in and cut the cords from its legs. It cowered in the corner and looked around for its mother. Harriet heated some canned milk, thinned it with water, added some sugar, and put the result in a baby bottle with a rubber nipple. Link took the bottle, crouched down beside the fawn, and invited it to eat. It was not interested.

"Squeeze a little of the milk out and smear it on the end of the nipple," Harriet advised. "Then hold it right up to the end of its nose."

Link tried for almost half an hour and then Harriet tried. Finally they gave up and had their dinner. After dinner Link tried again. This time the fawn finally drank about a third of the bottle.

"Success," Harriet said approvingly. "The main thing you need with wild creatures is patience. By tomorrow night, it will be drinking from that bottle as though it had all its life. I think wild animals know when someone is really trying to help them."

It rained the next day, and Charley Horse did not appear. There wasn't much else to do, and Link spent much of the day either feeding the fawn or taking its picture. As Harriet had predicted, it rapidly learned to drink from the bottle. Link saw what she meant about its becoming too tame. The tiny makeshift pen seemed far too small, so they let it wander around the main room of the cabin. It was soon following Link. When they went to bed, they again shut it up behind the barricade of boards. It didn't seem too happy, but after a final bottle, it curled up in the corner and went to sleep.

About four the following morning, Link woke with a start: something was licking his face. He rolled to the far side of his bed in wild alarm and fumbled for the flashlight that he kept on the little table. He had visions of a bear having forced its way into the cabin, but when he snapped on the light, there was the fawn, looking bewildered and frightened in the beam of light. He took it back to its pen where he found one of the boards pushed aside. He wedged this firmly in place with another chair and sleepily went back to his room.

He was just drifting off to sleep when he heard the noise of tiny hooves. The fawn was back again.

"Look chum, you may want to stay up all night, but I don't," he told the deer grumpily. This time when he returned the fawn to its pen, the board barricade seemed undisturbed. The fawn had either jumped over or had slid under one of the boards.

Maybe it was hungry, he decided. The fawn drank

hungrily and then went over in the corner and curled up to go to sleep. Link returned to his room, but by this time he was wide awake. He tossed around in his bed for half an hour and then went out and lighted the lamp again. He found the letter which he had written Pedro but had not yet sealed. He added a postscript to the back.

You'll never believe this. It's four in the morning, and the reason I am awake at such a crazy hour is that I have been feeding a fawn milk from a baby bottle. (A fawn is a baby deer in case a city slicker like you doesn't know.) It's a cute little thing. You'd think way up here in the boondocks people would drive a little slower because there certainly isn't any place anyone would want to go in a big hurry. But someone was going too fast and hit this little fellow's mother with his car. Her leg was broken so Charley Horse, he's the Indian with one arm, had to shoot it. I seem to be stuck with the job of raising the fawn.

He sealed the letter and went back to bed. He could picture Pedro reading that to his friends—probably at a baseball game because that was when they would all be together. It would create a sensation—it might even hold up the game.

5

The sky was gray and there was still a slight drizzle when Link awoke the next morning. He looked through his window at the misty weather and knew that Charley Horse would not appear. He turned over thankfully and tried to go back to sleep. However, he smelled bacon and coffee, and hunger won out over his sleepiness.

"Why were you prowling around in the middle of the night?" Harriet asked as she put on two eggs for Link.

"The fawn," Link said. "First it pushed aside one of the boards and came in and licked my face. The second time I think it jumped over the barricade. I finally had to feed it. Maybe we should build a pen outside."

"I agree," Harriet said. "It's getting too used to the comforts of civilization too fast. And I'm fast getting tired of cleaning up after it."

"The trouble is that we don't have any wire to make a pen or anything to use for a roof for a shed. I suppose it needs something to keep off the rain."

"It didn't have anything before we brought it inside," Harriet pointed out. "And it won't when it returns to the wild. You could probably make a small corral out of poles. And any sort of a lean-to with a brush roof would do for a shelter. The main thing is to keep it so it doesn't wander off into the woods and starve. I doubt if any animal is going to attack it this close to the cabin, especially since there will be a smell of man around the corral and shelter."

The sun came out about ten o'clock, so Link decided to build a corral. Harriet found a can full of large nails and spikes, and with these and an ax he began his building project. After he had cut a number of small trees and had lopped off their branches, he returned to consult Harriet as to the best place to build.

"I've never tried any carpentry work before," he confessed. "How about giving me some advice?"

He carried Harriet's folding canvas chair outside for her, and she sat down near the spot they chose for the pen. She was an excellent supervisor. She offered only an occasional word of advice, and that usually when Link asked her a question. She did not try to tell him how to make every move.

They selected eight small trees which Harriet said were of little or no value, and using these as posts for

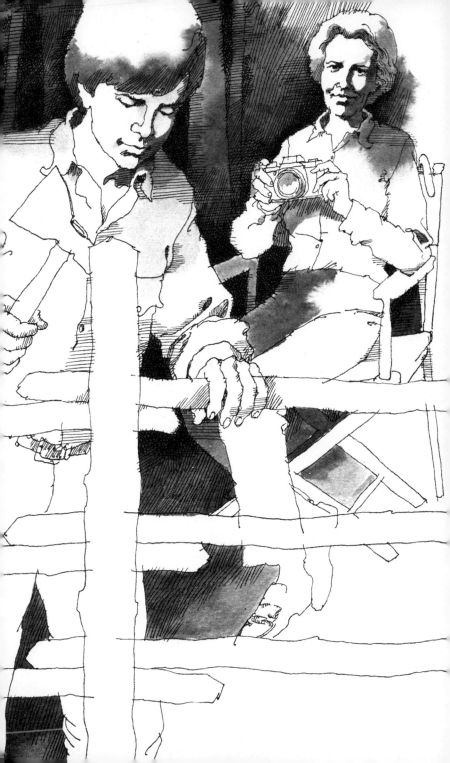

the corral, Link nailed his cut poles in place. By noon the corral was beginning to take shape.

"You should take some pictures of this, if it's your first building project," Harriet suggested as they ate lunch.

Link got his camera and loaded it with black-and-white film. He took a number of pictures when they returned to their project and gave the camera to his aunt to hold while he went back to work. By two he had completed the pen. Harriet gave him a brief description of how to build a lean-to and thatch it with the boughs he had trimmed from the trees. When he had finished he stood back and looked at his work proudly. He had every right to. It was a sturdy, workmanlike job. He went inside, got the fawn, and carried it to its new quarters. It didn't seem too impressed with all the work on its behalf and obviously would rather have stayed in the cabin. Link got the camera from Harriet's lap and took several pictures of the little spotted deer, poking its nose forlornly between the bars of its new corral. He finished the roll of film.

"Where can I get film developed?" he asked as he inserted a roll of color film.

"Any film for color slides or prints will have to be sent away," Harriet said. "However, I have to do some shopping, and I thought we might drive to Manistique. I know a man there who has a photographic lab—he prints film as a business. If he's in, he'll give us prints of any black-and-white film in an hour or two. I thought we might have dinner in Manistique to celebrate your finishing the deer pen. You did a fine job."

Link was used to his mother's effusive family, and a few days earlier he would not have realized that for Harriet "a fine job" was lavish praise. He felt pleased and happy as he put away his tools. He enjoyed working with Harriet. One of the reasons was that she wasn't at all surprised that he could do something like build a pen. She expected him to be able to do all sorts of things. That meant she thought he was intelligent and competent. Just as she was, he thought with pride.

He stuck four rolls of exposed film in his pocket and joined Harriet in the car. Manistique was not a large city, but it appeared huge in comparison to Germfask. Harriet stopped at a small cinder-block building near the business section and disappeared inside.

"They'll be ready by the time we've finished dinner," she said when she returned.

They went to a supermarket and bought groceries and supplies. Link found shopping with Harriet far different from shopping with his mother. Rebecca Keller loved food and liked to cook. Buying food was fun for her. For Harriet Keller it was a chore. She bought only the staples—bread, sugar, milk, bacon, eggs, ham, beans, and similar items found in every kitchen. Lincoln looked longingly at some of the items they passed by, almost drooling as he thought of his mother's meals. He knew if he mentioned anything, Harriet would quickly buy it. Having eaten her cooking for some days now, he also knew if they did buy some out-of-the-ordinary items, they would be ordinary by the time Harriet cooked them. Of course she was handicapped in that she didn't have much in the way of kitchen equipment at the cabin, but still his mother would have somehow made the food much more appetizing. He felt suddenly homesick. He hoped tomorrow would be a clear day and that he would be lucky. He'd find those crazy birds, photograph them, and head back toward civilization. His mother wouldn't be home, but he could go stay with any of his other three aunts. They were all good cooks.

They had dinner in a small café and then drove back to the photographic lab. Again Harriet was gone a few minutes. She returned with a bulky envelope.

"How much do I owe you?" Link asked.

"Nothing," Harriet replied. "Some of them are ones I took. I used one of your rolls of film so let's say we're even. Jim never charges me much anyway."

As they drove back toward the cabin Link looked at the pictures. The negatives of each roll, together with the prints, were in a separate envelope. The first several rolls were of the cabin, the spring, Harriet, Charley Horse, and of birds at the marsh and around the cabin. The pictures of the porcupine had been taken with color film and so were not there. The third roll had several shots he had taken of the fawn inside the cabin, a few of the deer pen partially completed, and then to his surprise a number of himself working. Harriet must have taken these. They were excellent photos—clear, sharp, and well composed. She must have moved around while taking them because a number could not possibly have been taken from her chair. The fourth roll also had some pictures taken by Harriet and then a number he had taken after completing the pen. The last one was of the fawn poking its nose between two rails of the completed corral.

"You took some very good pictures," Link said, shuffling back to look at them again.

"Thank you," Harriet said. "I wanted to get some of you that you could send to your mother."

If anything, Harriet's pictures were better than his, Link admitted grudgingly to himself. The thought was a bit upsetting. While his uncle's camera had a built-in light meter which indicated when the exposure was right, there was still some skill involved in taking a good picture. A fine camera was actually more complicated to operate than a simple cheap one, but of course it could take good pictures under conditions where a simple one could not. He looked at the pictures of the third and fourth roll again. Harriet had obviously finished the third roll, reloaded the camera, and had made ten or twelve exposures on the fourth roll. His uncle had spent half an hour explaining just how the camera was to be reloaded and warning him about things that could go wrong.

"Have you done much photography?" Link asked.

"I used to do some," Harriet said mildly. "Enough to be familiar with cameras."

Link returned the photographs to their envelopes and looked at the road ahead. His aunt was grimly concentrating on her driving, slowing at each tiny curve in the almost completely deserted road. She was a terrible driver and she was nothing special as a cook, but she was a surprising woman with a number of unusual abilities. She had a gun, and Charley Horse said she was an expert shot. His Uncle Al, who was a camera bug, had remembered Harriet immediately. That meant they had talked pictures. She had a close friend who owned a darkroom and would develop film for her on short notice. And the pictures she had just taken were excellent.

"What kind of a camera do you use?" he asked.

"A thirty-five millimeter," she said vaguely. "I've tried taking a few motion pictures with a camera I got a few years back, but I'm not agile enough to use it properly. One should be able to get down on the ground or climb a tree, if necessary, to get the right angle. You might like to try it. When you take your slides of the sandhill cranes, some motion pictures might be interesting too."

Charley Horse appeared about six in the morning. This time Link was ready and waiting with a lunch packed. Charley patted the seat beside him, so Link climbed into the Jeep. Dog leaped over the seat into the back and they went journeying down the lane.

"Going to Windy Lake today," Charley announced. "One of the State Police saw some sandhill cranes there the other day, and they're probably still around in the same general area."

"What did the police do with the deer?" Link asked.

"Gave it to me," Charley replied promptly. "I took it over to Munising to the freezer."

"You mean you're going to eat it?" For some reason it didn't seem quite right to eat the mother of his fawn.

"Sure," Charley said promptly. "Why waste it? We Indians believe it is all right to kill an animal when you're hungry. Of course we have to obey the white man's game laws. But even without the law, to an Indian it would be waste to kill a deer if it had a fawn that would die or to kill a buck just to stuff his head and hang it on the wall. I still have part of a deer that was killed by a car in February. Now that I have this one, it would be waste if I went out and killed a deer during hunting season."

"I suppose that makes sense," Link agreed.

"Handy things, freezers," Charley said. "Now if the white man had sold freezers to the Indians a couple of hundred years ago, there would have been fewer wars and fewer scalps lost."

Link was about to point out that there would have been no electricity to run a freezer two hundred years earlier, much less a freezer. Then he realized that the straight-faced Indian was kidding him.

"All right, why?" he asked.

"Because the Indian wouldn't have had to preserve his meat by making it into pemmican," Charley said. "My grandfather used to think pemmican made an Indian strong and brave, but I think it made him bad-tempered. My sister and I had to help my grandmother make pemmican, and what was worse we had to eat it. Ugh, heap bad, as your TV puts it."

How did you make it?" Link asked.

"We cut deer meat—or any kind of meat if you didn't have deer—into long strips and dried it in the sun. It was something like the white man's dried beef. This was pounded into a sort of pulp using stones. It was mixed with dried berries, and melted fat was poured over the whole mess. It tasted like a bad greasy sausage, but my grandfather liked it. My job was pounding the dried meat into shreds. One day I decided the white man had a better method, and I might as well use it. I had a friend send to Sears Roebuck for a little meat grinder. My grandfather said that was the best pemmican he had ever eaten and that I was very smart. He trapped all that winter, and with the money he made he sent me off to school."

"Where?" Link asked.

"Manistique," Charley replied. "Later I went to the University of Michigan."

They jounced along without talking for several miles.

So Charley Horse had gone to the University of Michigan all because he had bought a meat grinder. And because of a chance remark he had made at dinner in New Jersey, he was now in Michigan riding along with Charley.

"Funny how little accidents can change your whole life," he said after a while.

"Sometimes," agreed Charley. "But most of the time they just give you the chance to change it yourself."

They turned down an all but invisible trail into the woods. After half a mile they parked the car. As they walked, Charley pointed out various plants, shrubs, and trees that were sources of food. Link was familiar with blackberries and raspberries, but the blueberry bush was new to him. So were the wild leeks and the young ferns Charley said were called fiddlenecks and were delicious when boiled with venison.

"When there's frost there'll be beechnuts," Charley said, pointing to a beech tree. "But you have to get them before the bears do. The bears like blackberries, too."

After a fairly short walk they reached the edge of a marshy lake. Most of the surrounding area was flat and wet, but Charley managed to find a little hillock near the water's edge. They sat down under a blueberry bush to wait. The edges of the lake were choked with reeds, sedge grass, and bracken, but the center had some large areas of open water. The lake appeared to be several miles long.

"For some reason there have always been sudden

squalls of wind and rain on this lake," Charley said. "Especially at night. The Indians had a long name for it that meant 'Lake of the Spirit Who Cannot Sleep' "

They sat quietly for more than an hour. Charley Horse could sit absolutely motionless almost forever, Link decided. He kept shifting his weight, changing the position of his feet, and trying to get more comfortable. Charley moved only his eyes. Link had decided they were wasting their time when he heard a distant *yip*. Charley heard it too. He turned his head slightly and closed his eyes. Link heard nothing more but Charley evidently did. He got quietly to his feet and just as quietly headed back into the trees. Link followed.

"Dog has located something that has him puzzled," Charley explained. "I can tell from the way he yipped that he is excited. I hope he hasn't got a skunk."

They stood quietly for a minute, and this time Link heard the distant *yip*.

"That way?" he asked, pointing.

"I think so," Charley said. "No one can be too certain about sounds. You can stay here and wait for cranes or come with me if you want to. We won't be gone long."

"I need to stretch my legs," Link said, glad of anything to do other than sit.

Charley plunged into the tangled underbrush and Link followed. Link had learned by this time that the easiest way to keep up with the elderly Indian was to follow close behind him, stepping where he stepped and turning and twisting where he turned and twisted.

They made their way through the woods for almost half a mile, pausing now and then to listen. Finally they came out into a clearing. There was Dog circling warily around the end of a big fallen log. He would make half feints, back up a few feet, circle, and then give a puzzled little bark.

"Bear cub," Charley said. "That's odd."

"Bear cub? Where?" Link asked, excited.

"You can just see his head over the top of that log," Charley said pointing.

Link finally had to raise his camera and look through the lens to locate the spot of hair that projected above the log. "Can we get closer?" he asked. "I want to get a picture."

"We'll try," Charley said. "I don't understand why a bear cub should be alone. And if the mother bear thinks Dog, or we for that matter, might harm her cub, she could be dangerous."

They slipped cautiously through the woods and finally crept to within a short distance of the far side of the log. The cub was dark brown, almost black, and looked like a cuddly overgrown Teddy bear. Link took several pictures and then went even closer. The little bear seemed as puzzled by Dog as Dog was by him. Link got down on his hands and knees and, using a small bush as cover, finally managed to get within fifteen feet of the cub. Charley Horse stood motionless where he was, listening intently and warily eying the trees around the clearing. Link took a number of pictures. Then he shifted his weight and a dry stick cracked. The cub whirled in instant alarm, gazed at him in comical surprise, and then on all fours suddenly took off across the clearing.

Charley Horse said something to his dog, which had started off after the fleeing bear. Dog immediately dropped to a walk and waited.

"I think I hear something," Charley said. "If I'm right you'll see something not many people get to see."

With Dog leading, they went after the cub at a trot. Suddenly Charley held out his hand, and they all came to a stop.

"Listen!" he said, grinning with delight.

At first Link didn't realize what Charley wanted him to hear. It was a high-pitched angry buzz. Link raised his eyebrows in question.

"Bees," Charley said. "Mrs. Bear is robbing a bee tree."

They crept forward silently, and the buzzing grew louder. "You may get stung," Charley warned. "But still it will be worth it."

Suddenly Link saw the tree and the bear. About twenty feet up the trunk of an old oak there was a huge mass of black fur. A cloud of bees buzzed around its head almost hiding it from view. The bear was firmly planted with its hind feet on a big side branch and one forepaw circling the trunk of the tree. Its other paw was dipping into a dark hollow of the tree. It would come out periodically and disappear into an enormous mouth.

The bees were in a fury and were giving a good account of themselves. They seemed to be stinging the bear's nose and the area around its eyes. Now and then it would give a funny coughing roar of pain and swipe at its face to drive the bees away. But while the stings were undoubtedly painful, they were not painful enough to seriously interrupt the business of looting the tree of its honey.

There was a whimper, and they saw the cub struggling to climb up to its mother. The bear paused briefly and growled. Evidently it was encouraging its cub or scolding it for not climbing faster because the cub tried even harder. Its arms were not really long enough for the job but still it managed. A minute later it was on the branch beside the bigger bear.

The mother bear shifted slightly to let the cub dip into the tree hollow. The cub licked at something on the tree trunk and evidently liked it, for it stuck its paw into the tree. At that moment the bees discovered their new enemy, and a cloud of them surrounded the cub's head. The cub pulled out his paw, licked at it several times, and then gave a yelp of pain. It decided it had had enough and slipped quickly down the trunk again. It went running into the underbrush in a mad effort to get away from the angry bees.

"That's probably what happened before," Charley said. "There may be a second cub around someplace. They often have twins."

Link was not really listening. He was too busy taking pictures. The old bear was either much fonder of honey than its cub or more used to bee stings. It continued to raid the tree, pausing now and then to roar in anger and brush away a few bees. Link circled the tree, taking pictures from various angles. Finally he returned to where Charley was standing.

"I wouldn't have missed this for the world," he said happily.

"She seems to be running out of honey," Charley said. "And we'd better be gone before she gets down. She'll be looking for her cub and be in a bad temper from all those stings."

At that moment Link knew exactly what Charley meant for one of the bees discovered him and promptly stung him on the elbow. He made a wild slap at the bee, and two others began buzzing around his face. Evidently they found Charley, too, because the old Indian suddenly turned and scurried away. Link followed.

On their way back to the lake, they paused beside a wet boggy spot, and Link plastered his elbow with mud.

"The bear is probably doing the same thing," Charley said.

"Does a bear really know enough to put mud on a sting?" Link asked.

"It doesn't need to know much to do that," Charley pointed out. "The mud is cool and makes the sting feel better. Animals sometimes stick an injured paw in running water for the same reason."

"I don't see how that bear stood all those stings it must have got," Link said. "One sting is bad enough."

"The bear has a thick skin and maybe it doesn't hurt as much. I've seen a bear dip his paw into a yellow jacket's nest to eat the grubs. And a yellow jacket's sting is much worse than a bee's."

They returned to their bush and waited quietly for almost half an hour. The pain in Link's elbow began to subside and he felt sleepy. He was half nodding when Charley, whose sharp eyes never seemed to close, reached out to touch him on the arm. He pointed skyward. There were two specks in the clear sky.

"Cranes?" Link asked.

"Could be," Charley said with an expressive shrug of his shoulders.

The two specks circled and grew larger. Slowly they spiraled downward, gliding on set wings. Their necks were stretched out and their feet trailed straight behind. Charley looked at them carefully as they drew ever closer and then nodded and grinned triumphantly. They were cranes.

The two birds seemed to be playing in the air, side-slipping, twisting, and diving. Now and then they would change places, the upper bird diving to the lower position. When they did use their wings, they had a short upbeat and a long, slow downbeat. As they drew closer Link saw that they were enormous. Finally the birds decided they had wasted enough time, and they plunged downward coming closer and closer. They were great gray birds at least three feet long. They had long black legs, gray-brown bodies, white throats, long sharp bills, and red crowns.

The two birds lowered their long legs together and hit the ground together near the edge of the water. They landed with considerable speed and bounced several feet into the air, running a few steps and backstroking with their wings. They were enormous gangling birds with long spindly legs, but their movements were surprisingly graceful. Their bouncing hops as they landed gave Link the feeling that they must be equipped with steel springs. They both looked around warily, stretching their long necks upward and pointing their needle-like beaks into the air. They searched the area carefully, examining the shoreline as well as the water. Then they waded out a few feet into the edge of the marsh, walking with a strange jerky motion, their heads moving forward with each step.

Link watched the huge birds in fascination, forgetting his pictures until Charley cautiously touched him and pointed to his camera. Link raised it to his eye, focused it carefully, and tried to snap a picture. The button would not depress. The film was all exposed. He had used the last of the roll on the bears and had failed to check it.

"Nuts!" he said in disgust and reached in his pocket for a fresh roll.

His annoyed word was little more than a whisper, but

the wary birds heard. They raised their heads quickly and evidently saw his quick movement to get another roll.

One of the cranes gave a loud call of alarm. The cry sounded something like *garoo-a-a-a*. Almost immediately it was joined by the second crane in a slightly deeper voice.

"Warning call," Charley said and pointed upward. There circling downward were four more cranes. Hearing the call of alarm, they flapped their great wings and began climbing. Meanwhile the two at the edge of the lake took several running steps, seemed to bounce into the air, and began climbing rapidly. They were powerful fliers. In a surprisingly short time they were just specks in the sky.

"I certainly flubbed that one," Link said as he reloaded his camera. "What a dope. I'm sorry after all your trouble finding them for me."

"They came from that direction," Charley said, pointing. "They may have a roosting ground farther down the lake. But they won't go back until late this afternoon."

"Will they come back here?" Link asked.

"Not today."

"Then I guess I've shot the day," Link said unhappily. "We might as well go home. I've wasted enough of your time."

"No day in the woods is ever wasted as far as I'm

concerned," Charley said. "We saw the bear in the honey tree and that's worth a week of anyone's time. Some people go all their lives and never see that."

6

Link did not particularly enjoy admitting to his aunt that he had had an opportunity to photograph a sandhill crane and through no one's fault but his own had failed. However, he told her exactly what had happened.

"Of all the dumb tricks," he said in disgust as they ate dinner. "I was close enough to get a reasonably good shot, too. Charley Horse must think I'm a real dope."

"I doubt it," Harriet said. "Charley Horse has a great deal of patience. He knows that anything to do with wildlife takes time, particularly photography. And I daresay he has made his share of mistakes too."

"He never seems to make any in the woods," Link said.

"He grew up in the woods," Harriet reminded him. "People like us have to learn what is almost instinctive with him. Is it so terribly important to your uncle that you get these pictures? After all, you've tried."

"It's important to me," Link said angrily, half surprised at how strongly he felt. "I want to prove I can."

Harriet gave a short laugh. "Your father was stubborn too. Well, at least you have seen one now and also know in general where some are."

"I think I can find my way back there without Charley," Link said. "It's quite a hike from here though."

"I'm familiar with Windy Lake," Harriet said. "I can drive you part-way there. Do you mind if I make a suggestion?"

"Of course not," Link said. "I think I need a few."

"Cranes are early risers," Harriet said. "Shortly after dawn they start feeding. I imagine all their eggs are hatched by now, but the young won't be able to fly yet. So the adult birds and the young wade out, not too far from the nest, looking for food. Last year's young— they don't mate until the second year—fly from their roosting grounds to the feeding areas each morning. They may go five or six miles. In either case the best times to spot them are at dawn, about midmorning when they quit feeding and return to the nest or roost, about midafternoon when they go out to feed again, and then at dusk when they return for the night. So out of the four times of the day when you are most likely to see them, you miss two unless you are in the area before dawn and until almost dark. The simplest way to solve that problem is to camp overnight."

"That makes sense," Link said, wondering where one would sleep near Windy Lake. The only time he had camped overnight was at a camp where there was a lean-to that was almost a cabin, permanent fireplaces, and a pump for water.

"I have most of the equipment you'll need," Harriet continued. "All except a sleeping bag. You have a birthday coming up in August, so I'll buy you a sleeping bag now as a present if you'd like."

"That would be wonderful," Link said. He didn't have a sleeping bag at home and most of his friends did. He had doubts about how often he would use it for camping, but one was handy when visiting friends and there were not enough beds to go around.

As he thought about camping by Windy Lake overnight, he grew less enthusiastic. Carrying a sleeping bag, his food, a canteen full of water, his camera and lenses, a hatchet, and various other pieces of camping equipment would be quite a chore, especially through several miles of trackless woods. He would probably have to make two or three trips. Harriet was evidently thinking about the same problem.

"I know a better way of getting your gear in than carrying it," she said. "There's a small stream that crosses the road about three miles from here. It empties into Windy Lake. And I have a canoe."

"You have a canoe!" Link said. His aunt was a continual surprise.

"Yes, it's over at Charley's. I haven't used it for some

years, so I turned it over to him. He asked me the other day if you might like it for the summer. Do you know how to paddle a canoe?"

"I've paddled one several times but I'm no expert," Link admitted. "But I think I can get where I'm going. And I can swim."

"That's the important part," Harriet said. "Handling a canoe well is just practice. There's nothing terribly complicated about it. I have a friend I'd like to visit in Sault Ste. Marie, so I thought we might drive over there tomorrow and get you a sleeping bag. Wednesday we can get the canoe from Charley, and Wednesday night you could camp out at Windy Lake. I don't know whether you noticed it or not, but there's a small island toward the north end of the lake. It's a good spot to camp because you can see almost the entire shoreline from it."

Link looked at his aunt questioningly but her face told him nothing. Camping on an island in the middle of the lake was much more appealing than sleeping in the woods with bear, moose, skunks, and he had no idea what else wandering around. Charley had told him that moose were harmless except during the mating season when they got mean-tempered, and Harriet had said that bears seldom disturbed people if they were not disturbed themselves. However, he did not think he would feel happy stretched out asleep in the woods with wild animals blundering around in the dark. After all, there could be clumsy moose or bears just as well as people. Suppose one stepped on him by accident? And what about snakes? He had meant several times to ask his aunt if there were any poisonous snakes. Actually whether a snake was poisonous or not didn't make much difference to him. He hated them all, and the thought of one crawling into his sleeping bag in the middle of the night gave him cold shivers. However, this didn't seem the right time to ask about snakes.

"Have you ever camped out around here?" he asked.

"Oh, any number of times," Harriet said casually. As she continued, Link had the uneasy feeling again that she was a mind reader. "I was sort of scared the first few times I did it alone. I suppose everyone has his moments, hearing strange noises and thinking about wild animals. The only time I was really frightened was one night a wildcat yowled a few feet away from where I was sleeping. A cat gives a bloodcurdling screech that sounds like a person being murdered. I had heard it before, fortunately, but being awakened from a sound sleep by a screech like that practically beside me was unnerving, to say the least. It was five minutes before I was calm enough to realize what I had heard.

"About the only danger of camping out overnight comes from the camper. Too many don't build a proper fire, or else they leave it before making certain it's completely out."

"What about bugs?" Link asked.

"They're a nuisance," Harriet admitted. "In fact I would say insects are the one real pest of this part of the world. Some of those little flies can drive you mad in the woods. And there are mosquitoes. I'm glad you mentioned them. We must remember to get a piece of mosquito netting to put over your face when you sleep."

They left for Sault Ste. Marie after breakfast the next morning. It was about a hundred miles distant but the roads were practically deserted most of the way. However, Harriet drove her usual slow pace and worried the entire trip. It was almost noon when they arrived. They had lunch and went shopping for Link's sleeping bag, a tiny camp stove, and a few other items that he felt he needed. Then while his aunt went to visit her friend, Link went down to the busy locks to watch the ore and grain freighters pass through. He was surprised to find the U.S. Coast Guard in charge.

While Sault Ste. Marie was scarcely a large city, it was huge compared to anything he'd seen recently. Just seeing a traffic light gave Link a twinge of homesickness. Well, with a bit of luck and possibly a few uneasy nights in a sleeping bag in the open, he would have his pictures and be able to get back to New Jersey. He walked back to the business section of town and went into a store and bought a sheath knife. He'd probably need one, and besides it would look impressive when he got home and told his friends about his nights alone in the wilderness.

He met his aunt at four thirty, and they drove across the bridge into Canada so that Link could say that he had been outside the United States. It was still light when they got back to the cabin. While Harriet heated some frozen French fries and vegetables she had bought, Link grilled an enormous steak on a wood fire on the outside fireplace. Harriet ate only a small portion and Link, amazed at his own capacity, ate the remainder.

"One thing I'll say about the woods," he said as he finished, "It gives a guy an appetite."

"I suspect youth and all the walking you've been doing has something to do with it also," Harriet observed. "Anyhow, it's a good thing you're having a hearty dinner tonight. I've learned that I'm always half starved when I'm out camping. Even though I used to burn my food half the time, it always tasted delicious, and I never seemed to have quite enough. Of course campers today have it easy compared to my day."

"How so?"

"The equipment is so much better and so is the food. Take that tiny little camp stove you bought today. You can stick it in your backpack, and regardless of the weather you can have hot coffee or hot soup from one of those packages of dehydrated soup. You can build a simple little oven of stones and with a package of biscuit mix have hot biscuits or even a cake. And there's all sorts of little canned delicacies in the stores today."

"But no substitute for a fresh egg," Link observed.

He could gladly eat bacon and eggs for breakfast every day in the year.

"I agree," Harriet said. "When I was your age I felt I had to have eggs for breakfast, too. One time I made a special little box, all padded with cotton, that held two eggs. I went to a great deal of trouble. I put two eggs in it and went on an overnight hiking trip with a girl friend. I looked at the eggs when we arrived and they seemed fine. So I made a little stove out of a flat rock, and the next morning I built a nice fire and fried the bacon. Then I got out the eggs to fry them. Your father had hard-boiled them. I was furious. I hate boiled eggs."

"What did you do to get even?" Link asked.

"Several days later I caught a big fish," Harriet said, smiling at the thought. "A bullhead that was all slimy. I put it in your father's bed—way down where his feet would hit it."

It was noon the next day by the time Link had made all his preparations for his overnight camping expedition. They had lunch and drove over to Charley Horse's. It was the first time Link had seen the Indian's home. It was a neat white clapboard cottage set well back in the trees off a small clearing. There was a separate white garage and a small house that seemed to be a tool or garden house. He had a well-cultivated garden with an eight-foot wire fence around it.

"Gardening isn't easy around here," Harriet commented. "Deer will jump over any fence that's not high like that one. They like such things as lettuce and beans. And when the corn gets ripe, raccoons will climb over anything and steal as much as they can."

No one was home, but Harriet had expected that. Charley had sent word that he and his wife had gone to Minneapolis for a visit and to see a new grandchild.

"The canoe will be in the garage," Harriet said.

"Isn't it locked?" Link asked, getting out of the car.

"Very little is ever locked up here," Harriet said. "I doubt if his house is."

They found two canoes sitting upside down on two sawhorses. The canoe that Link had once used had been a bright aluminum with a fancy red and white stripe running its length. One of the ones in the garage was painted a dull brown, and the other an equally dull green.

"The green one is mine," Harriet said. "Charley and I argued for years about which color was better. I used mine more in the summer so I thought green was the least noticeable. He always claimed brown looked like a floating log to animals."

Link tied the canoe on top of the station wagon, found a paddle, and then he and his aunt set off down the road. About five miles from Harriet's cabin, she turned down a small trail for a short distance and was able to drive to within a few yards of a small stream. The water was almost dark brown. It was not wide but was several feet deep and would take a canoe easily.

"Some years ago when I last paddled down, it was clear all the way to the lake," Harriet said. "It's possible a tree may have fallen over some place and caused a jam. You'll either have to portage around it or clear it away in that case."

By the time Link had loaded his sleeping bag, his groceries, his camera case, a tarpaulin, and the other pieces of equipment in the canoe, he had quite a sizable load. Carrying it on his back in one trip would have been impossible.

"I want you to take my binoculars," Harriet said. "They're right under the front seat."

"I won't need them half as much as you will," Link protested. Harriet spent much of her day seated outside watching the birds through her glasses.

"Yes, you will," Harriet said. "It's difficult to tell from a distance what a bird is. You have to see the legs of a flying crane to tell it from a heron. There's only the barest chance a crane will land on your island. The most you can hope to accomplish the first few days is to find out where they roost or feed. Once you know that, you can camp some place nearer in the future."

Link felt guilty, but he took the binoculars.

"Good luck," Harriet said when he was finally ready to paddle off. "I have just one more piece of advice. If you hear some wild laughter don't be alarmed. There use to be a number of loons on Windy Lake."

They agreed to meet about five the next day, and Link

paddled off. A minute later he heard the sound of Harriet's car driving away, and then there was silence. The stream twisted and turned among the trees, and in a few minutes he seemed a thousand miles into the wilderness. The trees closed above him, and beneath him the brown water flowed quietly. It was like being in a dark, eerie tunnel. Suddenly he felt uncertain about the whole idea of camping overnight alone. How did he ever talk himself into such a crazy idea? he wondered. A shiver ran down his spine as he heard something slip away through the underbrush.

His canoe rounded a sharp bend and came out of the gloomy tunnel. The stream cut through a semi-clearing fringed with aspen and birch. He was being silly, he told himself sternly as the bright sun chased away some of his uneasiness. He had been out in the woods enough with Charley and by himself to know that there was little to fear. Harriet had probably known he would have his moments of uneasiness, he thought with a slight smile. That was why she had discussed her own camping trips as a girl. It was her way of telling him that if a girl had felt safe enough thirty years ago to camp in the woods, he could feel the same today. He slowly forgot about his qualms as his canoe glided along, and he began to see more of what went on about him. He startled one deer taking a drink, saw a sharp-tailed grouse slipping quietly through the weeds in a clearing, and watched a large snowshoe hare hop away unalarmed while keeping a wary eye on the canoe.

Link guessed it to be about five miles before the twisting stream left the trees and came out into the sunlight at the edge of the marshy lake. At first there was a narrow channel among the reeds and rushes, but soon this disappeared and he had to literally push his way through the rushes and sedge. The lake grew gradually deeper, and finally he found himself in open water. He paused and looked around to get his bearings. He finally had to use his binoculars to locate the little island that Harriet had mentioned. It was still several miles to the south on the long narrow lake.

It was almost five when he finally beached his canoe on the shore of the tiny island. One edge was muddy and covered with cattails and arrowhead, but on the opposite side he found a small sandy beach. He pulled his canoe up and hunted around for a good spot to make his camp. This did not need much thought because most of the island was low, wet, and covered with scrubby bushes. At one end there was a sort of hillock covered with jack pine and spruce. The ground was carpeted with pine needles. Link chose a spot and then noticed a small depression in the ground nearby filled with the ends of a few charred sticks. He had not been the first to camp there. He wondered if the fire could possibly have been built by his father on some camping trip long ago. Or if not his father, then his aunt.

He cut some spruce boughs and made a bed for his sleeping bag. He dug out the fire pit with a stick and gathered wood for a fire. He completely unloaded the canoe and carried all his gear to the campsite. By the time he had made all his preparations for the night, the sun was getting low, so he picked a spot under one of the tallest pines where he could see a good part of the lake shore and sat down to look for cranes.

Watching dusk come to the lake was a new and thrilling experience. A Canada goose came gliding in low over his head to settle some distance away among the reeds. A number of ducks he could not see well enough to identify came swooping over the trees about half a mile away and landed in the open water near the marsh grass. They quacked noisily for several minutes and then disappeared in the swampy grass. Still farther he could see a number of diving birds, fishing and sporting in the water. Some turned bottoms up and remained with their heads under the water for an incredibly long time, while other birds disappeared altogether as they dived beneath the surface. Strange calls sounded through the growing dusk. The western sky which had been a glowing red began to fade. Gradually the birds disappeared, and quiet descended over the lake.

Link put his glasses away and went to his camp. He lighted a fire and waited until it had burned down and then cooked three hot dogs over the coals. He heated some baked beans in a pot and half toasted and half burned some bread. Everything was delicious! Harriet was right again. After he had eaten and his fire had died down, he went back to his observation post although it was now largely a listening post. Eerie and mysterious noises floated out over the water, but he was used to them now and could even identify a few. Then the sky clouded over and the moonlight disappeared. A slight wind began to rise, and the night grew black. There was nothing to be seen and, with the sighing wind in the treetops, very little to be heard.

It was still not late, but Link decided he might as well go to bed. After all, he had to be up with the sandhill cranes at the crack of dawn in the morning. As he crawled into his sleeping bag he wondered if Uncle Albert had had any idea of what he had asked him to do. It had seemed such a simple request—just a picture of a sandhill crane. Link smiled to himself. If his mother and aunts and uncles could see him now. Aunt Alice in particular. She felt she was in the wilds if she got five miles outside New York City.

He drifted off to sleep, but some time during the night huge drops of rain on his face awakened him. He sat up in alarm and groped for his flashlight. It was not raining hard but the wind was blowing in fitful gusts, and from what little he could see of the sky, he suspected it was going to rain much harder. He found one of the sheets of plastic he had brought and carefully spread it over his supplies and his camera case. He fastened down the edges with some of the firewood he had gathered, remembering to put a few pieces under cover to keep them dry. Then he tucked the other sheet of plastic around himself, covering his head as well as the entire sleeping bag. In spite of the patter of drops on the plastic he drifted off to sleep.

He woke once much later in the night to hear the wind howling through the treetops. This was followed by a torrent of rain. He snapped on his light long enough to make certain that his supplies were still covered and then tried to get back to sleep. He lay awake for more than an hour before he finally dozed off. When he awoke the next time there was a pink light in the sky. Water still dripped off the trees but the wind and rain were over. He was much too warm with the plastic over him so he pushed it back, crawled out of his sleeping bag, and walked sleepily toward the lake. He had gone only a few feet when he stopped and stood motionless as an odd trembling call came floating across the water, breaking the morning quiet. He listened, fascinated. It did sound a bit like wild laughter, but it was more like a lonesome yodel. The notes were liquid, sad, and beautiful as they came trembling across the lake. He felt his spine tingle. He knew suddenly that the loon's call somehow expressed the spirit of the wild north woods better than any words ever could. He returned to camp and got his binoculars and went to his spot beneath the big pine and sat down. He tried to locate the loon. Although its haunting call came several times more, he could not spot it. He would sooner or later, he told himself confidently, and scanned the sky for cranes.

He sat quietly for more than an hour watching day come to the lake. Just as he was about to return to his camp for breakfast, he saw a giant bird appear above the cattails on the western side of the lake. The big bird was at least a mile away, but he was certain that it was a sandhill crane. He watched it climb high in the sky and then it began to circle, glide, bank, sideslip, and dive. Several times it climbed, and then finally it went diving and gliding back to the same general spot where he had first seen it. It landed somewhere near the water's edge and disappeared from sight. It had been much too far away for a decent picture, but he felt decidedly encouraged. Perhaps it had a nest somewhere over on the west bank. He picked out two especially tall trees as landmarks and went to get some breakfast.

He was ravenously hungry. Although several pieces of wood remained dry, he had no small twigs and was unable to start a fire. He had brought along his tiny camp stove with its canned heat, so he got that out and cooked two eggs and four strips of bacon. He made some coffee, drank it slowly, and then picked a spot where he could see another portion of the lake and sat down to watch again. He saw a number of Canada geese, several grebes, a bittern, and so many ducks that he lost count. He was able to identify the mallards and the redheaded male canvasbacks, but there were a number of others about which he was not certain. One little duck spent some minutes within a few feet of the island's edge, scooping up water and ooze with its oversize beak.

It seemed to be sifting the water through its bill and getting something which it ate. After consulting his book several times he labeled it a blue-winged teal but then changed his mind and decided it was a duck called a shoveler.

The morning passed quickly, and he forgot about time until his stomach told him it was noon. He returned to his camp and this time got a fire going. He made some soup and had that and a sandwich. He stretched out for a few minutes, enjoying just being lazy and alone. About one o'clock he decided an exploratory trip around the lake might be a good idea. He looked thoughtfully at his camping gear, and decided it would be safe where it was. Even if he did seem to be the only person within miles, he decided it was wise to take all his camera equipment with him. With the camera case and his binoculars he headed for the spot where he had left his canoe. He walked confidently down to the little sandy beach and stopped dumfounded. The canoe was gone!

For a moment he was panic stricken. Then he forced himself to sit down and think the situation over logically. It certainly didn't seem very likely that anyone had rowed or swum out and stolen his canoe during the night. What probably happened, he decided with a sinking feeling, was that he had not pulled it far enough up on the sand. During the night, the storm had made the lake quite choppy. The waves had lapped at the end of the canoe in the water and had floated it clear. Then the wind had blown it away.

He tried to remember the direction of the wind. It had been fitful and gusty but in general it had come from the northeast. He got out his glasses and searched the edge of the lake from the south through the west. Then he went to the other side and searched the north-western shoreline. Three was no sign of the canoe. The trouble was that the lake was long and irregular with jutting arms of cattails and sedge sticking out into the water where it was shallow. The canoe could be almost anywhere—three miles or only a quarter of a mile—hidden behind some of the marshy rushes. The long narrow lake had an outlet, he believed—a stream at the southern tip, he thought Charley had said. The canoe could be floating downstream on its way to Lake Huron or Lake Michigan, he wasn't sure where the stream ran.

He went back to his camp and sat down to decide what to do. He had seen no one, and he had been on the island since the afternoon before. Someone might appear at any moment but also he might sit there a month and not see another human. Not many people were crazy enough to be hunting for sandhill cranes, he thought sourly. He walked over until he could see the side of the lake from which he had come originally. The shore was at least half a mile away. The water was probably well over his head most of the way, but he didn't have much doubt that he could swim that far.

He went down to the water's edge and took off his shoes and socks. He waded out a few feet. Mud oozed between his toes, and the reeds scraped uncomfortably against his bare legs. He would no doubt be all scratched up by the time he reached open water. He didn't like the slimy ooze either, and he shivered as he thought of what might be hiding in the mud. But these were minor matters. The main thing that worried him was that the water was icy cold.

It was much too soon after lunch to try such a swim now, he decided. He might get a cramp. He went back, got his binoculars, and went to his lookout post beneath the big pine. He searched the shores of the lake, but he was looking more for signs of man than of sandhill cranes. It would be a long cold swim, he decided, and before he started out he should make a trial run. As soon as he was certain he had digested his lunch, he would go down to the little sandy beach and swim out a way. He would stay in the water a while to see how it was but not get too far from shore.

It was three o'clock before he finally made his test. He stripped off all his clothes and waded out a few feet. The water seemed even colder than before. He decided he might as well get the shock over at once. He held his breath and made a long shallow dive. By the time he had surfaced and had shaken the water from his eyes he felt half numb. There had been times when the ocean had felt unbearably cold, but after a few minutes the worst was usually over. He buried his head and began swimming away from the island with a slow, easy crawl.

He went out only a short distance and then turned. He swam around twice in a big circle, staying in the water at least ten minutes. The numbness never really disappeared, but he decided the water was endurable. He waded out and stood shivering on the shore, brushing the water off his chilled body and basking in the sun.

He could make it, he felt reasonably certain. Several things bothered him, however. He didn't like leaving the camera equipment behind. It would take hours to get ashore, trek through the woods to find help, and then get back with another boat or canoe. He supposed he could hide the camera case with all its lenses and the camera—dig a hole or perhaps put it up in the crotch of some tree where no one would be likely to see it. He thought briefly of trying to make a raft and pushing the camera equipment ahead of him as he swam. The case was probably watertight. He decided that would be silly. If he took anything with him it would be his shoes. After he did make it ashore, he would have miles to walk and going barefoot through the woods was not his idea of fun. However, even the shoes might be too much of a drag. After all it was a long swim for such cold water. If his feet got all cut up they would just have to get well again.

He returned to camp and took stock of his food. He had a can of corned-beef hash, some bread, two strips of bacon and coffee. He wouldn't starve. He would stay another night. He knew his aunt would worry and he was sorry. Tomorrow, if no one appeared by noon, he would swim ashore. He would wear only his shorts.

He had brought a fishing rod along, which he remembered late in the afternoon. He got it out, caught a beetle, put it on his hook, and made a cast out into the water. He had been surf fishing along the Jersey coast several times and at least knew how a cast should be made. To his amazement, on the fifth cast he had a bite. The fish put up a good fight, but a few minutes later he reeled in a nice-looking bass. Feeling quite proud of himself, he cleaned it, built a fire, and cooked it, holding it on a stick over the coals. It was delicious. He had two slices of bread and decided he would save his can of corned beef until the next day. It was too bad he didn't have a gun or a bow and arrow, he told himself as he drifted off to sleep. He could shoot a duck or goose and between roast goose and fried fish he could last indefinitely. The lake water was probably perfectly good to drink. This business of survival in the wilderness wasn't too difficult. Wait until Pedro and his other friends heard this story—marooned on an island and having to fish to keep from starving!

He was awake before dawn, and in the dim gray morning he did not feel quite so optimistic about his situation. He built up his fire and had a cup of coffee and one of his remaining slices of bread. Then he went

130

to his observation post. He watched the lake come alive and the various birds leave their nesting areas and take to the air. He heard the strange wild call of the loon. And again he saw a sandhill crane rise, circle high in the air, survey the lake, and descend. It came and returned to much the same spot as on the preceding day. Probably one of a nesting pair, he decided, remembering what Harriet had told him. The young were not able to fly yet, and so the parents were staying nearby. Then suddenly he saw seven cranes take to the air farther down the lake. They were at least a mile away when he spotted them, and they soon disappeared to the southeast. At least there were cranes on the lake. His camping trip had brought him that much knowledge even if it was pretty much of a mess otherwise.

He decided he would eat his can of corned-beef hash about ten o'clock and swim for shore about noon. About nine thirty he gathered some wood and got his fire going again. He was ravenously hungry and he enjoyed every mouthful of his meal. He finished his last half slice of bread and then walked slowly down toward the water. He wanted to pick a route that was reasonably direct but not blocked by too many reeds. He suspected it would be easier to swim than to force his way through too much swampy growth. He reached down and felt the water in the hope that suddenly it had become warmer. It hadn't. At least the sun was shining brightly and by noon the air should be quite warm. He was turning back toward his camp when he saw a speck appear in the open water several miles to the north. That was the direction from which he had come in his canoe. He rushed back to his camp and got his binoculars. As he hurried back to the north shore, he wondered what would make the best signal, to wave his shirt or one of the whitish sheets of plastic.

As soon as he could see the lake clearly, he raised his glasses. It was a canoe and someone was paddling it. It was still much too far to tell much about the occupant, but Link was certain that it was Harriet. Somehow she had loaded Charley's canoe onto the station wagon, unloaded it, and was coming to see what had happened to him.

She was quite a gal, Link thought happily. That must have been a difficult job, loading the canoe on top of the station wagon when she could hardly hobble around without her cane. And he knew her arthritis made lifting her arms above her head very painful. He supposed once she had the canoe waterborne and was in it, she was reasonably comfortable paddling. It was certainly far easier and faster than trying to limp through the woods.

The canoe was moving slowly in his direction. Link hurried back to camp and got his white sheet of plastic. He found a spot where he would be clearly in view and began waving it back and forth like a huge banner. Harriet was almost a mile away when she saw him. She raised her paddle high in the air for a minute and then lowered it. Link sat down on the shore and watched her move toward him. He felt better now that he didn't have to make that long cold swim, but he hated the thought of telling Harriet that he had lost her canoe.

She evidently knew the island well because she did not bother with the muddy north side but circled and came directly into the little sandy cove that Link had chosen. He had removed his shoes, and as she neared the shore, he waded out and grabbed the end of her canoe. He dragged the bow well onto the sand.

"Am I glad to see you!" he said.

"I'm happy myself," Harriet said with a small smile. "I was a bit worried, but I suspected that what happened was that you'd lost your canoe."

"Pretty dumb of me," Link said. "I didn't pull it up far enough."

"It's largely my fault," Harriet said. "I should have told you more about the lake. It wasn't named Windy Lake without reason. It seems to be in an odd pocket, and the wind here is stronger than any place around. The lake gets quite rough. There's a stream at the south end, but first the water has to be high enough to flow over a dam. A number of streams empty into the lake so when it rains heavily, even some distance away, the lake rises rapidly until it spills over the dam. So between the rising water and the wind you really have to pull your canoe well up or tie it to something."

"Do you suppose we can find it?" Link asked. "Wait a minute and I'll find a log or something for you to step on when you get out."

"I have some boots but I may as well stay put," Harriet said. "I find getting into a canoe isn't as easy as it once was. Arthritis is certainly a nuisance. Perhaps after we locate your canoe and come back I'll have you help me out. I'd like to walk around the island a bit. I used to consider it my private island. I once had a little shack on it so I could stay dry when it rained. By the way, I brought two paddles. Also there's a sandwich in case you're hungry. Bring the binoculars—we'll need those."

Link climbed in the bow and they headed down the lake. He alternately paddled and ate his sandwich. Harriet was unable to make any powerful sweeps with her paddle, but she was an expert. She kept the canoe on an even course down the middle of the lake.

"The lake doesn't seem particularly high, and I doubt if there has been enough flow over the dam to take the canoe with it. In fact I doubt if it ever reached the dam. It's probably caught in the reeds some place."

She was right, and they found the canoe bobbing up and down in a little pocket in the reeds near the southwestern corner of the lake. It had drifted at least two miles from the island. Link managed to get hold of the line in the bow, and they tied it on behind their own canoe and headed back up the lake. It was after one o'clock when they reached the island again.

"I had two steaks for last night," Harriet said as Link helped her out of the canoe. "When you didn't show up I decided to save them until today. They're in that package there. We might as well have them for lunch. It would be fun to have a meal here on the island again."

Link gathered some more wood and rebuilt his fire. Together they cooked the steaks. They had steak sandwiches, an apple, and some cookies for their lunch.

"I was going to swim at noon," Link said as they ate.

"The water is cold," Harriet said. "I've gone swimming here a number of times but only for a few minutes. Once I was in a little flat-bottomed boat on Lake Manistique and tipped over. I had to swim about a quarter of a mile, and I was half frozen when I finally reached shore. But it can be done."

"I wasn't worried half as much about the swim as the walk once I got ashore," Link said.

"That would have been difficult," Harriet agreed. "You did far the wisest thing—wait. One thing I should have told you was that if you get in trouble, make a big fire and put wet wood or reeds on it to cause a lot of smoke. There's always a sharp eye out for forest fires and any smoke is investigated promptly. But as it turns out, it wasn't necesary. Did you see any cranes?"

"Cranes, geese, loons, ducks, bitterns, and herons," Link said with enthusiasm. "The lake is alive with birds, and this island is certainly the place to see them."

"It's a good place to locate what's where," Harriet

agreed. "You will undoubtedly have to move to the shore to get any close-ups. But you're making progress, which is the important thing."

7

Link spent the next two days at the cabin, weeding and tying up tomato plants, feeding the fawn, and exploring the nearby woods. Either he moved through the trees with less noise, his eyes were sharper, or he knew what to look for, because he began to find much that was interesting in the same woods that he thought he had explored thoroughly his first few days. He saw raccoons and opossum, and near dusk a red fox slipped through the woods like a shadow. He discovered a hollow tree which was inhabited by a pair of owls, and a huge yawning hole that was almost a cave. It was half under a small ledge and half under a big fallen tree trunk.

"Probably some bear once spent the winter there," Harriet said. "They're very clever the way they find or fix a place for themselves. We don't have the caves around here that some areas do, so they usually have to do quite a bit of digging to make some hole or depression suitable."

As he prepared to go back to the island, Link discussed his plans with his aunt. "Which do you think would be the best to try to photograph, the pair or the flock of younger birds?"

"It's difficult to say," Harriet said. "The pair will probably be easiest to locate exactly since they tend to stay in one area. With their young having to walk as yet, they aren't apt to stray so far. Not that cranes can't walk fast. An adult crane can walk much faster than a man. But a young bird can't. The trouble is that cranes with young often feed in shallow water, and you would have to wriggle through mud and water to get close enough for a good picture if it's possible at all. Young birds are more erratic and they go farther to feed. It will be more trouble to locate their favorite feeding grounds. However, they often choose an open pasture or field. My suggestion is to see what the situation is with the pair and if that doesn't look promising try to find where the flock goes when it flies. In either case you'll no doubt have to build a blind to get your pictures."

"Blind?" Link asked. "What's that?"

"Some sort of little hiding place where you can see but not be seen. Duck hunters often use blinds. Well, photographing a bird requires much more skill and patience than shooting it. You have to get much closer.

The best blind for cranes is a low one. Find a sort of depression or dig a hole. Then camouflage it with reeds or branches. While cranes are very suspicious of man, they aren't as leery about blinds as crows. Crows can count."

"How does anyone know that?" Link asked skeptically.

"Observation," Harriet said. "If three people walk into a blind and then a few minutes later three leave, the crow knows the blind is empty and is safe to approach. But if only two leave, he knows very well one man is still there. I don't know how high a crow can count, but he definitely knows the differerence between two and three."

Link returned to the island in late afternoon and made camp in the same spot. However, this time he tied his canoe firmly to a tree. He saw no cranes at all at dusk, but the next morning at dawn he again saw the pair near the western shore and the flock take off. It again flew off to the southeast. He watched the black specks until they disappeared. Wherever they went, it must be at least five miles away, he decided.

He had breakfast and then paddled to the west side of the lake. He landed well away from the area where he had seen the cranes, beached his canoe, and then quietly made his way along the shore. There was a small shallow bay where the weeds and marsh grass jutted back into the woods. The two cranes were standing in about eight inches of water. They would dip their long dagger-like bills into the water and come up with something edible. Link was not certain whether they were getting some sort of root or catching small fish. Every few seconds they would raise their heads and gaze around suspiciously. At first he saw no young birds and then he heard a shrill *"peeeep."* After several minutes he managed to locate the source of the sound. A gangling, long-legged young crane was on the semidry land a short distance away. It seemed to be catching some sort of insect. It was light gray like its parents, but where the backs of their heads were red, its was a rusty, tawny color. There were also tawny patches at its wingtips and the ends of the tail feathers.

The two cranes moved closer to the young bird, apparently feeling it was getting a bit too far away. Link sat quietly watching them. He could see quite clearly, but he was much too far away for a good picture, even with a telescopic lens. As he watched they moved quite close to the higher ground on the other side of the little swampy inlet. Link studied the trees carefully. If he had a blind not too far from that clump of bushes opposite and if the cranes moved a little farther in that direction, the conditions would be just right for good photographs.

Link lay stretched out on the ground, watching quietly. He had his camera ready in case the cranes should decide to come in his direction. He took several shots, but he knew they would show little more than two distant long-legged birds standing in the water.

Suddenly the larger of the two birds leaped high into the air and landed gracefully in the shallow water. Then it bowed, almost touching the water with its bill. It raised its long swordlike bill straight up, turned slightly, and bowed again. It did this again and again until it had bowed in all directions. Then it leaped into the air again, rising above the water five or six feet. Its wings were half spread and its legs dangling and partly bent. For such a gangling awkward bird, it was surprisingly light and graceful. It alternately leaped and bowed, making a complete circuit. The other crane watched this dance quietly as Link watched in amazement. It was like a strange ballet with the crane bowing politely in all directions as though surrounded by a cheering audience. Several times during his higher leaps he fanned the air slowly with his wings and whirled at the same time. When he finally stopped, he seemed a trifle dizzy. Then he and his mate stalked away through the reeds in the direction of the one young bird. Link felt like clapping to let the crane know that he very much appreciated such a fine performance. However, he lay quietly watching while the cranes went still closer to the spot he had half picked for his blind.

The cranes fed, walked, and made short hops around the little inlet until about ten thirty. Then all three walked behind a particularly thick clump of reeds and disappeared. Link waited about half an hour and then paddled out into the lake a short distance and came back on the other side of the inlet. He found that the clump of bushes he had seen from the opposite was on a jutting point of land that stuck well out into the marshy inlet. It was almost covered with elderberry bushes, wild rose, and buttonbushes. He went some distance away and cut several additional shrubs with his sheath knife. He took these back to a spot where he would have a good view and added them to the bushy growth already there. He arranged them carefully to make certain he would be well hidden.

Link returned to his island, cooked lunch, and loaded his gear into his canoe. If he got his pictures, there would be no need to come back. He picked a tiny stream a short distance from his blind and dragged his canoe up-stream until it was almost hidden by the thick shrubbery. Then with his camera and several lenses he slowly and quietly made his way back to his blind. He crawled the last part of the way, staying hidden beneath the bushes so that if the cranes were within sight they would not see him.

One thing he was learning in Michigan, he told him-self as he sat waiting, was how to sit quietly. Even the longest study periods in school didn't compare with the hours he had sat waiting to take a picture of these long-legged birds. He almost chuckled aloud as he thought of how ridiculous it would sound if he tried to tell his friends how he had spent most of his time in Michigan— getting up before dawn, sitting under bushes for hours, going without breakfast while he looked through bi-noculars—all in search of a sandhill crane.

It would be impossible to explain to anyone how he had gotten involved in this crazy project or why he hadn't chucked the whole mess long ago. But the longer and more difficult the job became, the more determined he was to get his pictures. And now that he had seen that crazy dance, he'd like to get that on film. Those silly birds must have a sense of humor to go through such a crazy routine. Harriet had volunteered to let him use her movie camera. He wished now he had brought it along. However, if he could get a number of stills of the bird in the air, leaping, and then bowing, it would do. He hoped it would come back and repeat that dance.

He sat quietly until almost three in the afternoon, watching the lake, the trees, and the sky. Water birds circled and landed on the open water or in the marshes, songbirds darted from limb to limb through the trees at the edge of the forest. Blue jays quarreled noisily, joined now and then by chattering squirrels. Long hours of quietly sitting and watching, with nothing more to do than to look up birds in his bird book had produced results. He was rather proud of how many birds he knew by sight now—red-winged blackbirds, prairie marsh wrens, grebes, bitterns, terns, bobolinks, rails, meadow-larks, grackles, flickers, cowbirds, swamp sparrows, mourning doves, and dozens of others. He would astound his Uncle Al when he got home. It was odd, but Uncle Albert's slides, which used to bore him, would be interesting to see now.

Shortly after three a crane appeared overhead, circled

several times, and then flew away. A few minutes later two adult cranes appeared, walking through the cattails and sedge. A short distance behind came their one fledgling. Link's book said that cranes usually had two eggs in their nests. He wondered if one had failed to hatch or if something had happened to one of the young.

The cranes fed as they walked along, now and then giving a low-pitched call that sounded like "*purrr*" to Link. Suddenly one of the older birds gave a much louder call: "*Garoo-a-a-a.*" The young crane mysteriously vanished, and the other old bird stood stock-still. This was plainly some sort of warning, and Link wondered for a moment if they had seen him. However, they did not seem to be looking in his direction, and after several minutes they apparently decided it was all a false alarm. They again made the much softer *purrr* sound, and the young crane came out from hiding.

During the next half hour the cranes worked slowly closer to where Link lay. He checked and rechecked his camera and took two distant shots. However, he wanted to save his film until they got much nearer. The larger of the two adult birds was in the lead, walking toward Link in erratic, jerky steps. He had almost reached the point Link had picked as the limit for taking pictures when there was a sudden sharp report, like a gunshot. Where the sound came from, Link could not tell. The big bird in the lead gave a sudden start, staggered, and gave a cry of alarm. "*Garoo-a-a-a.*" It was echoed immediately by the second adult bird, which took several running steps and soared into the air. Link didn't see just what happened to the young crane, but it disappeared completely. The first big crane took two wobbly steps, flapped his wings, and took off uncertainly. His wing motion was uneven, and he did not soar upward as his mate had done but seemed to be having trouble gaining altitude. He flew directly toward Link. When he was almost overhead, he suddenly went into an awkward dive, crashed into a nearby bush, and fell to the ground a few feet away.

Link looked at the fallen bird with a mixture of amazement and anger. Someone had shot it! It gave two feeble kicks of its long spindly legs and then lay still. Link felt his rage rising. He'd like to get his hands on whoever had fired the shot. Cranes were good eating, Charley had told him that. Someone evidently didn't care that they were scarce and protected by law. All the hunter was interested in was a cheap dinner.

Whoever had shot the crane would undoubtedly come looking for it. He must have seen it fall. Well, he wasn't going to find it, Link decided suddenly. There wasn't much that he could do for the poor bird, but at least he could see that the hunter didn't get it. He slung his cameras over his shoulder and picked up the limp bird. Holding it under his arm, he crouched down and made his way through the underbrush. The crane, although between four and five feet tall, was not heavy. It weighed ten or twelve pounds at most. As soon as he was protected by the woods, Link hurried along at a dogtrot toward his canoe. When he reached it, he put the crane down and sat down to rest and to decide what to do next.

He hadn't given any thought of what to do with the crane except that he was determined not to let the person who had shot the bird have it. He had about decided to put it in his canoe and to take it home to show Harriet when suddenly the bird stirred. Link looked at it in amazement. It had been completely limp and lifeless while he was scurrying through the woods. However, he hadn't really examined it. Maybe it wasn't badly hurt and could be saved. He stepped forward to look at it more closely when it raised its head. It half sat up and looked around groggily.

"Where'd he hit you?" Link asked in a soothing tone and reached out a hand toward the bird's neck.

To his surprise, the crane made a sudden vicious jab at Link's hand. Link jerked back just in time. The long pointed beak went into the soft dirt at least two inches. A jab like that could go right through a person's hand, Link decided, drawing back to a safer distance. The crane got groggily to his feet, flapped his wings a couple of times and made a few menacing jabs in Link's direction. It was recovering astonishingly fast. Then Link remembered his camera. By the time he had removed the lens cap, the crane had headed toward the lake. He hurried after it.

It was only a short distance to the edge of the water. Link managed to snap one picture as he chased after the big bird but he knew it would not be especially good. It was too dim under the trees and there were too many branches in the way. With each step the bird seemed to be steadier. It reached the edge of the trees, took several springing steps, and soared into the air. It climbed with surprising speed and was soon well out over the lake, flying strongly. Link watched it rising higher and higher in the air. Finally it was only a speck.

Link stared after the disappearing bird. The entire episode was a puzzle. The bullet must have just grazed the big bird and stunned it. How else could it have recovered so quickly and completely? Yet he had seen no sign of blood, not even a scratch. Maybe some nerve had been hit and the bird was unconscious for a few minutes but not hurt at all. He would have to ask Harriet about it. Maybe she would know the answer.

He returned to his canoe and began paddling toward the stream he used as his entrance to the lake. He might as well forget about that hiding place. After being shot at, the cranes would certainly not go back to the same spot again. Once more he had almost got his pictures but at the last minute had failed. This time he did not feel so bad. The failure wasn't his fault and at least he had saved the crane. He would be no one's Sunday dinner. The big bird would no doubt find his mate. He would soar and glide and whirl in the air again and he would dance his crazy dance.

He saw no one as he paddled up the lake. He made his way up the small creek arriving at the usual meeting place well ahead of the time he was to meet his aunt. While he waited, he planned his next move. He supposed he would have to start all over again, watching from the island. Probably the best thing was to try to discover where the bigger flock went each day. The pair, now that one had been shot, would be doubly wary.

He told Harriet his afternoon's adventures as they drove back to the cabin. She listened quietly until he had finished. Then to Link's surprise, she chuckled.

"I suspect there's been a misunderstanding," she said. "You're annoyed because someone tried to shoot one of your birds, especially just as you were going to take its picture. And I suspect someone in the federal or state wildlife service is very annoyed because a crane he wanted to examine and went to some pains to anesthetize mysteriously disappeared.

"Anesthetize?"

"I think so," Harriet said. "There are little drug-filled darts which can be shot from a rifle. The dart hits the animal or bird and in a minute or so it's unconscious. Then it can be examined, marked, measured, and so forth. After a few minutes it wakes up and goes on about its business, none the worse. I've seen it done with bears. They use a drug called sucrestin on them. I suppose they use the same thing or something similar for birds. I've never seen drug darts used on birds, but I suppose it can be done on any large bird like a crane or a goose. It would certainly make sense with something as wary as a sandhill crane. I imagine it is a bit tricky, hitting a bird in a spot where the dart will go through the feathers and pierce the skin. I suppose the breast area would be what one would aim for. There's only down there."

"That could explain things," Link admitted. "It tried to fly and actually got off the ground. Then it conked out and practically dropped in my lap."

"It sounds like it to me," Harriet said. "And you say it was unconscious for a few minutes and then flew off. The dart probably hit it but dropped out some time before the bird got to you. The fact that you didn't see any blood and it had no broken legs or wings fits too."

"Well, I certainly messed up his plans, whoever he was," Link said.

"He messed up your plans for a picture, so you're even," Harriet said, laughing. "It's too bad you both didn't know what the other was doing. He could have waited until you got your pictures and then you could have got several close-ups of the unconscious bird as well."

"Is there any chance the cranes will go back to that spot?" Link asked.

"I doubt it," Harriet said. "I'm afraid you will have to start over and find their new feeding grounds. There's a thing called Murphy's law: Everything that can go wrong will go wrong. I guess that's the case with your pictures of sandhill cranes."

"It seems that way," Link agreed. "But one of these bright and shining days they will go right, and then I'm going to get some beautiful pictures. I saw one of the cranes dancing today. I want a movie of that. Otherwise no one would ever believe me if I told them about it."

"It's wonderful, that dance," Harriet agreed. "It's rather unusual to see a pair with young dancing. When they are in bigger groups they dance much more often."

"Then I'm going to locate that flock of seven that goes off somewhere to feed each day," Link said.

He waited two days before going crane hunting again. He and Harriet spent one day shopping in Manistique and one day reading and writing letters. A number of letters arrived for both him and Harriet, some forwarded from Melton and others that had come direct to Germfask. Most important to Link were three letters from his mother—two to him and one to Harriet. The first letter was largely about her computer school. It was full of bubbling enthusiasm. Link could almost hear his mother's voice as he read it. She was apparently doing well and enjoying herself. He was almost annoyed that she seemed to be having such a good time. While she said she missed him, there wasn't the slightest hint that she'd like to be back home. The second letter was in much the same vein, but it contained the news that she hoped to get a four-day weekend later in the month and would fly up to see him and Harriet.

Harriet's letter evidently contained much the same news. "Your mother sounds quite happy," Harriet commented when she had finished her letter.

"Yes, she does," Link agreed. "I was afraid she might be homesick."

"She probably misses you much more than she lets on, if that's what you mean," Harriet said with a sharp look at him. "But you might as well face the fact that your mother needed a change. For the past twelve years since your father died she's been pretty much tied down taking care of you and working. I've never been a mother, but I daresay they need to get away from their children just as much as the children need to get away from them. A change of scene, a change of routine—it's amazing what they can do for one. This is a vacation for her. Where do you think she'd prefer to come, to my house in Melton or up here to the cabin?"

Link had been thinking of a weekend someplace with some modern cooking facilities. He knew that he could wangle matters so that Harriet would step aside and let his mother do at least part of the cooking. Link thought longingly of a dinner of roast stuffed veal, scalloped potatoes, a cheesecake for dessert, or perhaps a big apple pie. And for breakfast, waffles or an omelet and pop-overs. His mouth watered. Then he remembered what his aunt had just said. This was his mother's first vacation in years and spending a weekend cooking might not be what she'd like. Also if they went to Melton, it would mean a day's drive down and a day's drive back at the speed Harriet drove. If he added the four days his mother would be visiting, the total was six days, almost a week. While he was certainly buried in the wilderness up here at the cabin, there was much more to do than there would be in Melton. He could show his mother through the woods, perhaps even take her out to the island.

"I think she'd enjoy it here more," he said. "This would be a real change. I doubt if she's ever stayed any place like this."

There was a letter from Pedro. Link read it eagerly but was somewhat disappointed. Pedro informed him that their baseball team had won four games, lost two, and had been robbed of one by an unfair umpire. Life was pretty much the same in New Jersey, Link decided, and nothing very exciting had happened. Pedro must not have received his letter about the porcupine because he failed to mention it.

There was also a short letter from Uncle Albert. Link had dropped him a note some time earlier saying that he had seen his first sandhill crane and hoped to have a picture soon.

DEAR LINCOLN:

I received your letter and am glad to know that you have located some sandhill cranes. However, locating them and getting a good picture are two different things unless you are much bettter sneaking up on things than I have ever been. However, don't be discouraged if you have trouble. I'm enclosing $10.00 in case you need more film. If you've already been successful and have the crane pictures, try to get me a slide of a pied-billed grebe. They're an odd little water bird, very interesting to watch in the water. I think they nest up there in the summer. This isn't too important because they also migrate through this area. I've seen them at the Brigantine Wild Life Refuge, but they're very shy. I've never been able to get close enough in eight or ten years of watching to get a good picture. My best regards to your Aunt Harriet.

Hope you are enjoying yourself.

REGARDS,
Uncle Albert

A few weeks earlier Link would have gone into a fit of laughter at Albert's interest in a bird called a pied-billed grebe. Now he knew exactly what Albert meant. It *was* an interesting bird. It was the one that could sink and rise like a submarine. After several nights on the island he also knew its call. All day and sometimes into the night it said, "*Cow-cow-cow-cow-cow-cow-hu-cow-hu*" when it was undisturbed. As a matter of fact, he recalled rather proudly, he already had several pictures of a pied-billed grebe. He had taken them the day of his accident with the porcupine.

The last but not least items in the mail were several packages of color slides. Harriet had sent them off as he had taken them. The service was surprisingly fast. There were some of the cabin, some early shots of songbirds, a few of the old beaver dam, and several very good slides of the pied-billed grebe. These were followed by a number of excellent close-ups of the porcupine in the tree. Link could almost feel the pain as he looked at the spiny creature. Another set of thirty-five were of the bear cub and the mother robbing the honey tree.

Since they had no electricity, a projector was out of the question. Link and Harriet took turns looking at each slide through a battery-illuminated viewer. Harriet was enthusiastic about them all, but particularly about those of the bears.

"You could try a lifetime and never have another chance to get pictures like that," she said. "With a little script to tell the story, you could make those into a filmstrip that would be excellent."

"For who?" Link asked.

"You're talking to a schoolteacher," Harriet said. "*Whom*, not *who*. But to answer your question—for almost anyone. How many people do you know who have ever seen a bear outside a zoo, much less one robbing a honey tree! What I have in mind are school children some years younger than you. Teen-agers would probably enjoy it, too, if they'd let themselves. By the time a boy or girl is your age he pretends he's interested only in the opposite sex or cars. He thinks he's too sophisticated for bears and duck and lambs. But young children are honest—they like any kind of animal, tame or wild."

"Sounds pretty complicated, making a filmstrip and recording sound to go with it," Link said doubtfully. "I'm having trouble enough just getting plain ordinary pictures of a sandhill crane."

"Believe me, there is nothing plain or ordinary about a picture of a sandhill crane or a bear in the wild," Harriet said. "Neither one stands and smiles and poses like your pal or girl friend does. A filmstrip really isn't so difficult or complicated. When you get your pictures of the cranes we'll talk about it if you're interested."

Link looked through the pictures again. One thing he liked about his aunt was that she didn't harp on a subject. She made a suggestion and let it go at that. These bear pictures *were* good, he thought proudly as he looked at one of the mother bear swatting furiously at bees.

"Did you ever take any pictures of bears?" he asked.

"Some," Harriet replied. "I lost a camera trying to get some close-ups of a mother bear and two cubs." She limped over to look out the window. She gave one of her rare chuckles. "It wasn't too far from here. I remember it well. It was my first good camera and it took all my savings to buy it. I had one good lens, a fifty-five millimeter as I recall. What I should have had was a telephoto lens like the one you have. Anyhow, to get the pictures I wanted, I got too close to the bear and she came after me. I ran. I knew that the bear could probably run faster than I could, and so when I saw a good tree with a branch about the right height, I jumped, caught the branch, did an up-and-over the way I'd been taught in gym class in school, and then kept on climbing. Bears can climb trees, of course, but they're at a disadvantage when the trunk is small and smooth. This bear didn't do more than make motions toward climbing. My camera was hanging around my neck, and I must have torn the strap getting up on that first branch. Anyhow, the strap let go and the camera dropped. It hit one of the few rocks around and at the worst possible angle. The lens was cracked and the camera itself bent so badly it was ruined. The only thing that was any good was the film."

"It makes me feel a little better to know that I'm not the only one who has had trouble getting pictures," Link said. "Maybe I haven't been so unlucky after all. At least all of Uncle Albert's equipment is still in good shape. I don't know how I'd ever live it down if I wrecked his precious camera. And it was plain luck I didn't when I fell out of that porcupine tree."

8

On Tuesday afternoon Link gathered enough supplies for two days, and Harriet drove him to the little stream.

"This time I'm coming back with pictures of sandhill cranes," he promised as he loaded the canoe. "If I'm real lucky I might be able to locate their feeding grounds tomorrow morning and get some pictures in the afternoon. In that case I may hike back. But the chances are it will take me all day tomorrow to locate the spot and build a blind. Then the next day I'll get the pictures."

"Then I'll be back about five o'clock day after tomorrow," Harriet promised. "I should go shopping some time tomorrow, so if you do get back and I'm not there, I'll be along shortly. Good luck!"

Link paddled downstream to the lake and then went four or five miles to the southern end of the long narrow strip of water. He found a suitable spot to camp and dug a shallow pit for his campfire. He had spent enough nights in the woods so that he no longer gave a thought to his early fears of being disturbed by bears or a moose. He was willing to believe Charley's advice that the wild animals were far more anxious to avoid than to bother him. The same wasn't true of the insects, however. For some reason, probably the breeze that usually blew on the island, the bugs there hadn't bothered him too much. They made up for it at his new campsite. He had to swat at gnats continuously while he cooked his dinner, and later as he sat watching by the lakeside, he finally put a piece of mosquito netting over his head. He had brought some insect repellent, but as far as he could tell the buzzing gnats liked the flavor.

Aside from the bugs, his campsight turned out to be well located. Shortly before dark the flock of sandhill cranes came flying over the lake from the southeast. They circled and dropped down to the water not more than half a mile away. Link thought about sneaking along the shore to discover their resting area, but it was growing dark fast and he decided to stay where he was.

He went to sleep early, setting his tiny traveling alarm clock for four in the morning. When it went off he struggled awake and, still half asleep, cooked breakfast. Then he tidied up his camp, made certain the fire was completely out, and stowed his camp gear in the canoe. He kept a small hatchet in a leather sheath on his belt and hung his binoculars over his shoulder. He put his still camera, the movie camera, a supply of film for both, and one sandwich in his knapsack. Then he carefully dragged the canoe out of sight in the underbrush and set off to the southeast. By the time it was half light he was at least a mile from the lake. He picked a tall beech on the edge of a clearing and climbed up until he had a reasonably good view in all directions.

He did not have long to wait. The flock of cranes appeared from the direction of the lake, flew almost directly over his head, and continued on to the southeast. He watched them fly for about three miles, then they spiraled downward and disappeared. The countryside was too flat, and Link was not high enough to see where they landed. All that he could tell from that distance was that the spot where they landed was either open land or the trees were short and stunted. There was little to use as a landmark, so he made a careful note of the direction on his compass, climbed down, and started out.

He made his way slowly and carefully through the woods, enjoying the wildlife as he went. There were a number of small natural clearings in the trees, and Link approached each of these as quietly as possible since the cranes could be feeding in any one. Also he had learned that such clearings were the best place to see animals and birds. For some reason they seemed to like the conditions at the edge of the trees. He saw grouse, two deer, countless songbirds, and a porcupine sound asleep in a hollow log. Along the banks of one small stream which he crossed, there were several freshly cut trees, signs that beaver were at work nearby. Link made a note to come back later and explore the stream. Some pictures of a beaver actually gnawing down a tree would be interesting, although he didn't know how he would go about it. They did their tree cutting at night, Charley had told him.

He saw no cranes in any of the small clearings that he passed. He was beginning to wonder if he had come too far or was too far to the right or left, when suddenly the forest thinned and he found himself on the edge of a large area of open land. A few scrubby trees grew here and there, but the land had obviously once been cleared completely and used for some kind of farming. Link stayed cautiously in the shadow of the trees and looked carefully over the open area with his binoculars.

There were two large fields that he could see, each at least half a mile square. They were separated by a thin, straggly line of trees and the remains of a split rail fence. Link searched the first field thoroughly but saw nothing that resembled a crane. He carefully skirted it, staying hidden in the trees, until he could see the second field.

It turned out to be considerably larger than the first, and the far end was low and swampy. There, almost in the center, were seven long-legged sandhill cranes, stalking around on their stiltlike legs. Every few minutes they made sudden jabs with their beaks at the weed-covered ground, apparently catching insects. One bird, much nearer the marshy area, seemed to be probing with its long pointed beak for some sort of root. All of them raised their heads every few minutes to look around warily.

Link weighed his chances of crawling near enough to take a picture. The abandoned fields were covered with weeds, tall grass, occasional clumps of bushes, and here and there a seedling tree. Whatever the area had been used for, it was just beginning its long slow way back to forest. The cover was too spotty, he decided. The sharp-eyed cranes would spot him long before he could get close enough. The safest and best course was to wait until they flew away and then build a blind. He picked a spot where he could lean back against a tree and sat down to watch and wait. About ten thirty there seemed to be some sort of a signal. Almost together the cranes ran a few steps, bounced into the air, and climbed rapily upward. They turned and headed back toward Windy Lake.

Link waited until they were out of sight and walked to the center of the field. They had seemed to favor the part of the big field nearer the boggy area, so he located a convenient clump of bushes. It was a good start, but the cover was not thick enough to hide him well. He cut a number of other shrubs from the far side of the field and added them to the clump, sticking the cut ends into the ground to make them look as natural as possible. When he had finished, he looked at it from every angle. He even lay on his back in the center of his blind to make certain that he could not be seen from above when the cranes flew in to land.

He glanced at his watch. It was only a few minutes after eleven. The cranes would not be back until about two thirty or three, if they came back that afternoon. He would spend the time exploring and trying to locate a beaver dam. He considered leaving his knapsack with the heavy movie camera but changed his mind. Anything could happen and he might not get back that afternoon. He decided to walk straight west for one hour. If his guess about the stream he had crossed earlier was correct, he would hit it again, only farther upstream. If he found nothing, he would simply reverse his steps and come back.

He had hiked for almost forty minutes when suddenly he came to a lane or trail leading through the trees. It was about the same size and showed about the same use as the one leading from the road to Harriet's cabin. Since it was going in the general direction that he wanted to go, he decided to follow it. It was easier walking than pushing his way through the underbrush.

He had followed the tiny road only a short distance when he suddenly came to a large clearing. Only this clearing was not an overgrown farm field; it was filled with a cluster of buildings. The old road he was follow-

164

ing left the trees, headed across the clearing, and disappeared between two rows of low, weathered frame structures. On the side of one of the larger buildings there were the remains of a painted sign. The letters had half peeled away, but the words were still quite readable: "Sutcliffe Timber Industries, Inc."

There was an eerie quiet about the clearing. Even the birds seemed to be making less than their usual noise. Nothing moved. The breeze, which had been so pleasant in the fields Link had recently left, was missing here. An old logging camp, Link decided, walking slowly toward the gray weatherbeaten buildings. And it had been a huge one—practically a city.

He slowly made his way across the overgrown field until he was in the middle of the sprawl of buildings. One long low building, open on three sides, was obviously a sawmill. The huge circular saw was still in place as well as the ancient steam engine that had once driven it. Both were covered with rust. A veritable mountain of sawdust rose behind the building. At first Link was uncertain what the enormous mound was because it had long since partially decayed, and its surface was covered with weeds and grass. A few stacks of half-rotted lumber and a big pile of slabs that had once been the outside of logs were nearby.

The sawmill was at one end of a street bordered on both sides by low buildings. One building with a square false front had a faded sign that said it was the general store. A smaller building nearby had the remains of a red cross painted beside the door, indicating that it had been the first-aid center, among other things. Link pushed open the sagging door of the next building, a long low structure, to find it filled with wood tables and benches. This was evidently the mess hall; the kitchen was at the far end. The other buildings were bunk-houses, he decided, as he walked slowly down the weed-choked street. And those smaller buildings that looked like houses were probably where the married workers lived with their families.

Near the end of the street, one building on the right seemed in much better shape than the others. The roofs of some of the bunkhouses had sagged, but this roof looked as though it might still shed rain. As Link got nearer he saw a faded sign hanging from an iron bracket sticking out above the door. It said "Main Office" and beneath in smaller letters, "Paymaster." As he walked closer he saw that the windows were still intact. He was about to peek in the nearest one when a sudden voice sent a tingle up his spine.

"Stay right there!" it warned. "Put up your hands."
Link did as he was told.

"Now lower your right arm slowly and take that bag off your shoulder and drop it on the ground," the voice ordered. "Don't turn around."

Again Link followed the orders exactly, too fright-ened to even think of anything else. There was a slight

rustle behind him, and the knapsack disappeared from where he dropped it. There was a short silence and then finally the voice said again, "Now you can turn around. Slowly and no tricks!"

Link turned to see a short stocky man about ten feet away carying a double-barreled shotgun. He was wearing a pair of old gray trousers and what had once been a white shirt but now so dirty that it was almost gray. His beefy face was topped by a battered felt business hat that was creased and greasy and as dirty as the shirt. The man had suspicious pale blue eyes, a stubble of white beard, and a very ample stomach that stretched his trousers tight and made the bottom of his dirty shirt gape.

"What are you doing here?" the man demanded.

"Nothing," Link said when he could find his voice. The man was holding his shotgun in his right hand, now and then waving it around carelessly. Link didn't know much about guns except that they were dangerous and shouldn't be waved like batons.

"Nothing! Ha!" said the man in a scornful voice. "That's a camera on your shoulder isn't it? And binoculars!"

"Yes," Link said with a sinking heart. The man already had the knapsack with his aunt's movie camera and all the film.

"Taking pictures of my operations," the man said. "That's what you're doing. I'll bet my competitors sent you. Just like them to send a boy. Thought I wouldn't be suspicious of someone your age."

"Look, I'm just trying to take some pictures of sandhill cranes," Link said. "I haven't taken any pictures around here at all. I was just looking, honest. I've never seen a logging camp before."

"Well, you're seeing one of the best now," the man said, his tone changing suddenly from suspicion to pride. "One of the biggest and the most efficient in all the Upper Peninsula. Millions and millions of board feet of fine lumber have been shipped out of here." Then he looked at Link again suspiciously. "This all is private property, and I don't allow trespassers. Who told you how to get here?"

"No one," Link said. " I was just hiking through the woods hoping to find a beaver dam."

"A likely story! First it was cranes and now it's beaver. You're talking to L. P. Sutcliffe the Third, my boy, and I don't fool so easily." He reached down and picked up Link's knapsack where he had dropped it. He motioned toward the door of the office with his shotgun. "We'll go inside, and I'll see what you've got here."

Link looked longingly at the trees, but they were much too far away. Sutcliffe had a shotgun and he seemed just wild enough to use it. Slowly and reluctantly, Link walked toward the door. How had he got in this scary mess?

"Open the door and go right on in," Sutcliffe said behind him.

The inside of the office was a complete surprise. Most of one long wall, except for two windows, was covered with bookshelves. Every inch of shelf space was filled with books. The opposite wall was covered with framed photographs. There was a small flat-topped stove near the back of the room with a few pans on it. Evidently this was Sutcliff's cookstove and probably his heat in winter. There was an open cupboard with some cans and cartons of food on the shelves. Not too far from the stove were two chairs, a small table with a kerosene lamp, and a narrow steel cot with a thin dingy-looking mattress and a dingier blanket. A blue business suit hung on a wire hanger from the edge of one of the book-shelves. Beside it on a second wire hanger was another white shirt. It was far cleaner than the one Sutcliffe was wearing—it was only grimy. These were probably Sut-cliff's best clothes which he wore for special occasions, Link thought.

The front end of the big room still contained what were probably the original furnishings. There was a big roll-top desk crammed with yellowed papers and en-velopes, a high bookkeeper's desk, a stool, and a small steel safe.

"Sit down," Sutcliffe ordered, waving his hand, still holding the gun. He pointed in the general direction of the cot and chairs. "And stay there while I look through this bag."

Link obediently sat down while Sutcliffe dumped out his knapsack on the top of the bookkeeper's desk. He merely glanced at the movie camera, but he picked up one of the rolls of film and said, "Aha! Pictures you took of my camp."

"Those aren't even exposed. You can look and see!" Link protested.

"Spies," muttered Sutcliffe. "I'll keep these." He gathered the rolls of film together, both the extra movie film and the thirty-five millimeter, and turned around. He tugged on the safe door once or twice and then gave up. He dumped the film into a drawer of the roll-top desk and slammed it shut.

"Honest, I've just been taking pictures of birds and animals. That film hasn't been used." Link said.

"You like pictures do you?" Sutcliffe asked suddenly. "Take a look at those on the wall. Now there's some pictures for you. They really show something. My competition would like to have those!"

Link got to his feet and went over to look at the pictures, hoping to be able to edge nearer the front door. The entire wall was covered with photos of the camp when it had been a bustling, thriving logging operation. Some had turned brown and a few had faded, but most were surprisingly clear. There were pictures of the saw-mill in full operation, great sledges piled high with logs and drawn by heavy draft horses plodding through deep snow, bearded loggers swinging their sharp axes, men high in tall trees, topping them out. One picture showed a huge group of men gathered in front of the mess hall. One was wearing a white apron, but all the rest appeared to be lumberjacks. There must have been at least a hundred men in the camp at the time the picture was taken.

"A lot of men worked here," Link said, looking at the picture.

"This was one of the busiest and finest camps in all of upper Michigan," Sutcliffe said. "Those were the days! The sawmill was busy all day, teams hauling logs in from the woods, other teams hauling boards out to the railroad. Look at the picture up there to your left. No, over two or three—see that big team of oxen pulling that load of logs? They're Alphonse and Gaston, two of the finest animals the north woods ever saw. They won every pulling contest they ever entered. They were a legend here in the logging country. I wouldn't be surprised if this camp and that team of oxen didn't have a lot to do with the stories of Paul Bunyan and his great blue ox, Babe. Ever hear of them?"

"Yes," Link said. "What happened to the camp? Why did it close?"

"Why, all the trees were cut down," Sutcliffe said in an injured tone as though someone had suddenly pulled a dirty trick on the company. "I'm all that's left. The lumberjacks, the teams, the trees, everything—all gone."

He sat down on a chair and stared at the floor. He was still holding the shotgun in his hand, however. Link edged slowly toward the front door.

"What's your name and where are you from?" Sutcliffe asked, still not raising his head.

"My name is Lincoln Keller and I'm staying with my aunt, Harriet Keller, at her cabin," Link said.

"That woman!" Sutcliffe shouted in a sudden rage. "She interferes with everything I try to do. A meddling busybody!"

Link decided it was wisest to say nothing at all.

"The trees are gone but they'll come back," Sutcliffe said almost plaintively. "They're growing up all around here, and soon there'll be timber like there used to be. The camp will be busy again, the sawmill will run, and the Sutcliffe lumber company will have jobs for hundreds of men again. We'll send out timber to the cities to build fine houses, if the meddling busybodies will just let me. But all they care about is geese. People and jobs for people can go hang. Geese, geese, geese!" He put his gun down on the floor and buried his face in his hand and began to sob.

"I think I'll go now," Link said, but Sutcliffe did not seem to hear him. Link reached over, grabbed the movie camera and his knapsack from the desktop. His thirty-five millimeter camera and binoculars still hung over his shoulder. He opened the door softly and stepped outside. Sutcliffe continued to sob behind him. As he hurried down the deserted weed-choked street he realized that he was trembling. He felt weak and tired, but he knew this was no time to stop and rest. When he reached the point where the trail came out of the woods, he paused long enough to take one quick look behind. There was still no sign of Sutcliffe. The logging camp with its sagging buildings was deserted and quiet. A few more years and it would be gone like the forest it had once devoured.

"That guy was a lunatic," Link said aloud, getting some comfort from the sound of his own voice. "I was scared stiff!"

He missed the spot where he had first entered the trail and suddenly found himself on a narrow graveled road. He stopped to decide what to do. The trail to the logging camp had been quite straight, and Link had little doubt that he could find his way back to the two fields and his blind without retracing his route exactly. Then he remembered his extra film. It was back in the desk drawer at the logging camp. With Sutcliffe and his gun still there, Link had no intention of going back after it. Both cameras were loaded with fresh film, and that would be enough if he were lucky. He glanced at his watch. Time had passed faster than he thought, and it was probably too late to get back to his blind before the cranes appeared for their afternoon feeding. The sensible thing to do was to go home where he had more film and plan on taking his pictures in the morning. He tried to remember the map of the area. It would be faster to go home via the road than to return to the canoe, paddle the length of the lake, and then make a long hike through the woods.

He had walked perhaps an eighth of a mile down the road when a dark blue sedan appeared behind him. Link had learned that almost every motorist offered every pedestrian a ride in the backwoods, so he was not surprised when the car stopped. The driver was a dark-haired, pleasant-faced man. He rolled down his window and asked if Link wanted a ride.

"We're headed toward Germfask, I hope?" Link asked.

"That's right."

Link climbed in the front seat and sat down gratefully. He suddenly felt tired and weak. He had been more frightened by Sutcliffe than he realized at the time.

The man glanced at Link's camera. "What are you taking pictures of?" he asked.

"Nothing, it seems," Link said. "I've been trying to get some pictures of sandhill cranes, but everything goes wrong."

"Join the club," said the man. "I've been trying to band a number of them, and I haven't been having much luck either. They're suspicious, wary birds."

"How do you get close enough to band one?" Link asked, his tiredness forgotten.

"I have a dart gun. There's a drug on the end of the dart that knocks the bird out for a few minutes, or is supposed to. The only one I've got close enough to hit so far flew a short distance and then dropped some place where I couldn't find it."

"Was this over by Windy Lake?" Link asked.

"Yes. How'd you know?"

"Because I was trying to photograph that bird," Link said with a grin. "I guess we messed each other up."

Briefly Link explained what had happened. " I haven't tried to find out where that pair is now, he said. "But I have located where the flock of young birds feeds."

"They're the ones I'd like to band," the driver of the car said. "Look, I'm Dan Olson and I'm with Fish and Wildlife Service. We're trying to get some reliable information on migration patterns of the sandhill cranes. We're banding them, or trying to, I should say, with a bright band we can spot some distance away with glasses. we use a different color for each general nesting area. Anyhow, it appears we could both accomplish more if we worked together. Would you show me where this flock feeds if I promise to let you get your pictures before I try to band any of them?"

"Sure," Link said. "I've got a blind all built. I might have got my pictures this afternoon if I hadn't been held up," he laughed. "Held up is right. Held up and robbed of my extra film."

"What do you mean?" Olson asked.

"Do you know anything about a strange character who says his name is Sutcliffe?" Link asked.

"Oh, old Sutcliffe Timber Incorporated," Olsen said with a laugh. "Yes, I know him. "He's a bit off."

"He's a real kook for my money," Link said. "He

held me up with a double-barreled shotgun and accused me of being a spy from his competitors."

"He's harmless, really," said Olson. "And that gun isn't loaded. In fact it doesn't even have a firing pin. The State Police check on him and his gun regularly. Most people around here know him and they don't let him bother them. You say he took your film?"

"Yes, that's why I'm going home now—to get some more," Link explained. "I know I've got extra thirty-five millimeter film and probably some for my movie camera. Then I'm going back and get my gear and camp out for the night. Tomorrow morning I'm going to be there when those sandhill cranes arrive."

Olson stopped his car. "Look, if you're making this trip just to get film, I'll take you back, and we'll get your film from Sutcliffe. Then you can show me where your blind is, and I'll be there well before dawn tomorrow morning to join you. Is the blind big enough for two?"

"I think so," Link said.

They drove back the way they had come and turned down the trail to the lumber camp. Olson drove his car up to the front door of the office. There was no sign of Sutcliffe or anyone else.

"He's probably out scouting his timber," Olson said with a smile. He pushed open the door and stepped inside. Link followed him. Olson walked over to the big desk and opened the drawers. The film was in the second one where Sutcliffe had dumped it. Link stuck it in his knapsack, and they returned to the car.

"What's wrong with him?" Link asked. "He told me all about what a great lumber camp this once was and then he broke down and cried."

"He's sort of sad," Olson said. "Actually he knows very little about the great days of this camp. They were over before he was born, Sutcliffe Timber Industries was a big outfit about eighty years ago when his grand-father ran a lumbering operation here. The camp was probably still operating in a small way and shipping some lumber when this Sutcliffe was a boy. But it's been closed down for at least sixty years. He's half confused between what little he actually saw and what his grand-father and father told him. The family made a lot of money, and this Sutcliffe went off to school and was in business in Cleveland. Somehow he lost everything, and he came back here and holed up in that office where he's been for at least fifteen years. He must be at least seventy. He owns about a hundred acres around the camp but half of the time he thinks he owns thousands of acres the way his grandfather used to. And he talks about starting up his sawmill again. But of course he can't. The big trees are gone."

"That's what he said. The trees are all gone. It *is* sad."

"It's sad in several ways," Olson said grimly. "Between 1870 and 1890 the entire Upper Peninsula was lumbered off. Millions of acres of some of the finest timber in

North America. There were beautiful stands of red pine, cedar, spruce, all the conifers. The lumber companies just cut everything in those days. No one tried to practice any decent land management."

"What kind of management?" Link asked. "If you cut down a big tree it's gone, and about the only thing you can do is wait until another one grows."

"You can plant new trees," Olson. "You can leave a few standing that will drop seeds. But the lumber companies stripped everything clean and often set open fires to get rid of the debris so that logging operations would be easier. If any of them gave any thought to the damage they were doing, they probably figured America had so much land it didn't make any difference. But of course it did. Even if man didn't need the land the birds and wildlife did—and not burnt-over land."

Link decided that they were about as close to his blind as they could get by car, so they parked and proceeded on foot.

"The underbrush has grown back, that's for sure," Link said as they threaded their way toward the clearing.

"Nature has a way of restoring things," Olson said. "But for a long time it had a tough job around here. Land development companies followed the lumber companies. They drained all the marshes and swamps and sold the land as farms to people who didn't know any better. Most of them went broke and moved away. The land was sold for taxes, and now finally it's back in the only sensible crop for the area—trees."

"There are some big trees around my aunt's cabin," Link said.

"There are some fine stands here and there," Olson admitted. "And of course you can't keep the whole country the way it was when the Indians roamed the land. We do have to have lumber. I'm happy to say that the trees are coming back and much of the wildlife. Nowadays most lumber companies practice reasonably good management. I suppose there will always be some who are ignorant the way the Sutcliffes probably were or who are just plain greedy." He stopped to point at a beer can. "Or slobs."

"I suppose if he was able to carry the full can in, he ought to be able to carry the empty one out," Link agreed.

"Certainly he could," Olson said indignantly. "Stopping pollution isn't just passing a law. Everybody has to work at it. That means the people who throw cans and bottles out of car windows, litter the woods, and burn trash in their back yards. I suppose I sound like a schoolteacher delivering a lecture. To change the subject, how did you happen to get interested in taking pictures of birds and wild animals?"

"An accident, mainly," Link admitted with a grin. "And while that lunatic was waving that gun around I was afraid it might be a fatal accident." He spotted the first of the two cleared fields through the trees. "We're getting close. I think we'd better circle around to the left."

They slipped silently through the trees until Link's blind was in view. There were no cranes.

"That's where they were this morning," Link said, pointing. "And I hope that's where they'll be tomorrow morning."

"They vary their feeding areas so you can never be absolutely certain," Olson said. "All right, I'll join you well before dawn in the blind. Let's hope the cranes come too."

Olson went off in the direction of his car, and Link started back toward his canoe.

9

Link cooked an early dinner at his campsite of the night before and then, with his sleeping bag and enough food for breakfast, he hiked back through the woods to a spot only a short distance from the big field containing his blind. He slept well and got up a short while before dawn and ate a cold breakfast of a banana, two pieces of bread, and a slice of cold ham. He would have liked a cup of hot coffee and an egg, but he did not want any smoke rising from a campfire to alarm the cranes. When he had finished he carried his sleeping bag out to his blind and made a comfortable spot where he could sit or lie while he waited. He had scarcely settled himself when Olson appeared. He had come up quietly, and Link had no idea he was around until he was within a few feet of the blind.

"You've got yourself set quite comfortably," Olson

commented as he sat down beside Link. "What did you do, sleep here?"

"No over there a ways, back in the trees," Link said. "There's a tiny little stream with some water."

"Have any breakfast?"

"Not much of a one," Link said. "I'm hungry enough already that I could eat one of those cranes."

"I brought along a big hunk of coffee cake," Olson said. He reached into a small knapsack he was carrying and brought out a package and a Thermos of hot coffee. "Thought you might like some. We might as well have it now. I wouldn't want you eating our cranes. You know they used to be on the menu at some of the hotels out on the Pacific Coast along about the turn of the century. Of course they are much too scarce to allow any hunting now; not that hunting made them scarce half as much as all the draining of the marshes and the crowding in of people. There used to be lots of sandhill cranes in Iowa, Wisconsin, and Minnesota, for example, but you never see any there now."

"A hunter would have to be pretty good to get one of these," Link observed.

Olson inspected and loaded his gun and Link checked his camera as the field grew lighter.

"Cranes eat seeds, berries, roots, worms, bugs, almost anything," Olson said. "My guess is that at this time of the year it's grasshoppers and bugs that they're after in a place like this. You'll want to wait until the sun gets up a ways so you will have good light for your pictures. They'll hang around for several hours if they come, so there's plenty of time."

"I hope they land near enough to our blind," Link said. "If they don't show up this morning, I'm going to wait here until this afternoon."

"You're determined, aren't you?" Olson said. "That's the only way to accomplish anything in this wildlife field. It took years before they could discover where the whooping crane nested. By the way did you know they used sandhill cranes as sort of test birds for the whooping cranes?"

"No, I didn't," Link said. "How?"

"The whooping crane was practically extinct," Olson said. "There was a lot of publicity on whooping cranes so you probably know that they are on the increase now. I think that everyone is pretty well agreed that the best way to save an endangered species, bird or animal, is to protect it from hunters, provide it with its natural habitat, and let nature take its course. But when a species gets as low as the whooping crane did, twelve or fifteen pair, one single disaster—for example, an oil slick in a nesting marsh—could wipe it out. So the Bureau of Sport Fisheries and Wildlife has a sort of backstop operation. It's at the Patuxent Wildlife Research Center in Laurel, Maryland. They're doing work on a number of scarce species—the whooping crane, the Florida kite, the California condor, the masked quail, just to name a few."

"What sort of work?" Link asked.

"Oh, they study a bird's nesting habits, what it eats, how many young it usually hatches, what conditions it likes best. The sandhill crane isn't exactly plentiful, but there are lots of them compared to whooping cranes. The two are much alike—sort of cousins. At Patuxent they study the sandhill crane to know how to best help the whooping crane."

"I'd like to visit the place," Link said.

"It isn't easy," Olson said. "The public isn't welcome. The place isn't a zoo in any respect, and they don't want the birds and animals to get used to having people around. They want to observe them as they act in the wild. There's canvas around the sandhill crane area, for example, so the cranes won't be disturbed by people. The actually have some whooping cranes, too."

"Where did they get them if they're so rare?"

"Hatched them. They learned that whooping cranes usually lay two eggs, but when the first one hatches the parents tend to go off and leave the second. So it's wasted. When someone finally discovered the whooper's nesting grounds in Canada, a joint Canadian–United States expedition was organized. The men went in by helicopter and got six eggs one spring. They took only one from each nest. They hatched the eggs artificially and raised four cranes from six eggs. They made another trip the following year and raised seven chicks from ten eggs. So then they had thirteen. I don't know how many they have now. Anyhow, they hope to raise enough so that they can release some into the wild. As I said in the beginning, everyone agrees that if a species can fight its way back naturally, that's far the best. But at least now if something terrible happened to our few wild whoopers, we'd still have a chance. The masked quail was completely extinct in Arizona, and the Patuxent Center managed to capture a few pair in Mexico. They've now released several hundred in their old range and are protecting them until they get well-established."

"That sounds like interesting work," Link said with enthusiasm. "Isn't there some way I could get in to see what goes on?"

"You might, if you wrote ahead and said you were interested in wildlife and conservation," Olson said. "Are you from that part of the country?"

"I live in New Jersey," Link said. "I'm visiting my aunt for the summer. She has a cabin up here. Her name is Harriet Keller."

"Harriet Keller your aunt?" Olson asked. "And here I am telling you about sandhill cranes. So that's how you happened to be so interested in photographing wildlife!"

"What do you mean?" Link asked.

"You mean you don't know about your aunt's work?" Olson asked.

"What work?" Link asked. "Before I came out here this summer I'd seen her only once. She came east to visit us. She's my father's sister, and my father died some years ago. I thought she taught in junior high school."

"Maybe she does," Olson said. "But Harriet Keller was with the Michigan Department of Natural Resources—one of the early people in the wildlife and conservation field for the state. She did some outstanding photography. Of course it was all black-and-white because color film wasn't fast enough for good animal snapshots when she did most of her work. There were a number of booklets and then some filmstrips issued using her pictures. She took some pictures of a bear and its cubs that are classic. That bear had to be chasing her when she took several of those shots. And she took a beautiful set of pictures for a filmstrip on sandhill cranes that is still the best available. Many of her filmstrips are still in use in school systems all over. Her articles and pictures did a lot to get people interested in saving some of our wilderness and the creatures in it. She was quite a gal. She's partly responsible for getting me interested in this work. I've never met her but I've always wanted to."

Link looked out at the field and the woods that surrounded it. So Harriet had been an expert wildlife photographer. She had photographed sandhill cranes—enough fine photographs to make a filmstrip. And not once had she tried to tell him how he should go about getting his pictures. Oh, sure, she had told him something about the cranes' habits and had answered any questions he had asked. She had known that he had to find them and take his pictures in his own way. He grinned. She hadn't warned him how difficult the job would be, or he would have gone home way back at the beginning. Aunt Harriet wasn't above a little bit of scheming either, he decided. She probably guessed he would finish the job once he started. She gambled all along on his taking so long that he would get to love the woods.

"I heard she was partially crippled," Olson said.

"Arthritis," Link said. "It's hard for her to get around to take pictures."

"I suppose she didn't want a desk job," Olson said. "Maybe she retired from her job with the state. I don't know the details. So she's teaching now? I'll bet her pupils end up knowing more about wildlife and conservation than most."

They heard a distant "*garoooa*" and fell silent. A few minutes later the cranes appeared. The big birds circled over the larger field twice, and then they started downward. They were flying in a formation of three, two, and three. Suddenly the rear three swooped down under the others and took the lead. Then all of them made a quick turn to the right, then to the left again. The middle two passed through the spaces between the three in the lead, who dropped back. Finally they seemed to tire of the game. They dived downward steeply and landed with considerable speed, taking several bouncing steps and flailing the air with their wings.

There were eight of the big gangly birds. They scattered and looked around cautiously. Then they began to feed, jabbing at the ground with their long sharp beaks. Link and Olson sat watching quietly as the light grew stronger. The largest of the birds was at least four feet tall when its head was raised. It had an almost black beak and legs, ashy gray back and wings, somewhat paler gray breast and stomach, a featherless forehead, and a crown that was bright red.

The cranes stalked around haphazardly, making darting stabs for insects, but always raising their heads high every few minutes to look around carefully. After almost three quarters of an hour one started in the direction of the blind, feeding as it came. Link had been ready for some time, keeping his camera focused and changing the exposure as the light grew stronger. Using his telescopic lens he began snapping pictures. He took almost half a roll of the feeding bird, some with its head raised high and some with its long beak almost touching the ground. He put down his camera and picked up the movie camera. Olson tapped him on the arm.

"Wait," he said soundlessly, his lips forming the word rather than saying it. He pointed to the other birds. They were all moving in the direction of the blind.

A few minutes later the cranes had formed a circle about ten feet in diameter only a short distance from where Link and Olson were hiding. They faced inward and for a minute or two did nothing. Then one leaped into the air, hopping upward and slightly backward. It

flapped its wings and landed a foot or so from where it had been. Then it solemnly bowed to the circle of cranes, facing first right and then left. Link raised his movie camera and began recording the dance on film.

A second bird dropped one wing, another raised a wing. Then one crane reached down and picked up a stick in its long, sharp beak and tossed it high in the air. As the stick fell, the crane gave a leap into the air, whirling slightly as it rose. It landed gracefully, bowed to all the others and then repeated the whole performance. Gradually they all joined in the grotesque dance. They did not leap into the air or bow together but moved as the mood seemed to strike them. First one and then the other would leap and bow or toss sticks and bits of weeds into the air. Sometimes there would be two or three in the air at once. Some would dance a moment and then soberly watch the others. The whole performance lasted not quite five minutes. Then as suddenly as it had begun, it stopped.

Olson looked at Link and raised his eyebrows. Link put down his camera and nodded. He had been afraid that the sound of the filming might reach the dancing birds, but apparently they had been too excited to notice. Olson raised his rifle and fired three times in quick succession. At the first crack, the birds sounded a wild alarm and all started to take off. Two did not get off the ground, and the third flew only a few feet before it dropped.

Olson raced out of the blind with Link close behind. Olson stopped at the first two birds, while Link ran on to the one that had fallen a short distance away. Olson had given him some broad canvas straps. He fastened a long one around the body of the crane, pinioning its wings, and put a shorter one around its legs just above the feet.

Olson quickly banded his two cranes. "If it starts to show any movement, get back," he warned Link. "That beak is dangerous. It can put an eye out."

He banded all three birds and made a quick inspection of each one. The birds were still limp when they removed the straps. Link changed lenses and snapped several pictures of the unconscious cranes, lying stretched out on the ground. He took several close-ups of their head, and then he and Olson returned to the blind.

They did not have to wait long. The three birds began to stir. First they got groggily to their feet and staggered a few steps. Then one sounded a call of alarm. They all ran a short distance and took off. As they climbed they seemed to gain strength. When Link and Olson last saw the big birds they were tiny specks in the sky, heading back toward the lake.

"A very successful morning, I'd call that," Olson said.

"I can't believe it! I finally got my pictures!" Link said. "And some good ones, I think."

There were only two exposures left on the still camera, so he took one picture of Olson and one of the blind.

Then he rewound the film. Uncle Albert ought to be happy with some of those shots, he thought as he put the roll of film carefully inside its little aluminum container and then in his knapsack. He'd slept any number of nights on the hard ground, got up at four in the morning, been marooned on an island, and been threatened by a lunatic with a shotgun. But he'd got the slides for Uncle Albert's collection. Visitors would drop in and Albert would proudly show his slides. And when he came to the sandhill cranes, one or two guests might ask what that odd-looking bird was and that would be all. Link grinned. It didn't matter that none of them would know what a triumph that slide or two was. He knew. He'd set out to do something and he'd succeeded. He'd found his sandhill cranes.

"Can I give you a ride anywhere?" Olson asked.

"No thanks. I have to go get my canoe and other gear." Link said. "My aunt is going to pick me up later this afternoon."

"Here's a bar of chocolate that I won't be needing," Olson said. "Why don't you look me up at the Seney Wildlife Refuge? I can take you where you can get some fine pictures of Canada geese and a number of other water birds."

"That sounds interesting," Link said. "I'll be over."

"I'd like very much to get a print of that film of the dance if you can arrange it," Olson said. "If you'd let me know how much it will cost, I'll give you the money."

194

They shook hands and Link hiked off through the woods. He found his canoe with everything just as he had left it. He paddled up the lake, landed at the island and cooked lunch there. He had two eggs left, and so he had bacon and eggs for lunch. He even toasted his remaining three slices of bread, and he had the chocolate bar and some dried apricots for dessert. It wasn't quite up to the standards of one of his mother's Sunday dinners, but it was good. He stretched out and took a nap for half an hour. The sun was warm so he went for a quick dip in the lake. Then about four in the afternoon, he got in his canoe and lazily paddled toward his meeting place with Harriet.

He arrived at almost the same moment as she did. She got out of the car and came limping down to the stream bank.

"Well, how did you make out?" she asked.

Link raised his hand and made a *V* for victory. "I think I got some beautiful pictures! And I got a movie of a whole circle of cranes doing that crazy dance of theirs. It was wonderful!"

"Great!" Harriet said. "I'm anxious to see it. I don't think any one has ever filmed a good crane dance."

Link began unloading his camping gear. When he reached his camera, Aunt Harriet, who was standing on the bank, held out her hand.

"Here, I'll take that," she said. "I'm not much good at carrying things, but at least I can take good care of something like that."

Link handed her Albert's camera. He bent down in the canoe and got the movie camera. As he stepped from the canoe to the bank his foot slipped on the mud. He gave a giant step, lost his balance, and fell sideways against his aunt, who was standing about a foot from the edge of the stream. The blow was just enough to throw her off balance, and she pitched forward. She jabbed at the ground with her cane but it slipped on the muddy bank. She dropped the cane and fell forward into the canoe. She tried to cushion her fall with her right hand, still clutching the camera tightly with her left. She landed across the thwarts with a gasp of pain.

Link jumped down into the water beside the canoe. Harriet's feet were in the water, and she was struggling to get up. Link put his arms around her and helped her stand. Her face was white with pain.

"Here," she said, holding out the camera.

Link put the camera safely on the bank. If she had dropped it, she might have been able to catch herself. Instead she had held onto it at all cost.

"What did you do, hit your ribs?" he asked.

"I hit my ribs but not hard enough to bother," she said. "It's my wrist that's bothering me."

Link helped her ashore and then over to the car. She sat down in the passenger's side of the front seat, her face glistening with perspiration.

"I'm feeling a little woozy," she said. "Just let me sit a few minutes."

He went back, found her cane where it had fallen in

the water, and returned with it. He loaded all the gear in the car and put the canoe on top.

"How do you feel?" he asked, when he had finished. Her color was slowly returning.

"I'll live," she replied with a faint smile. "But I think I've cracked something in my wrist. I don't know how I'll drive."

"I can drive," Link said confidently. "I may not have a license, but I can drive." He got behind the wheel and started the motor.

"Charley is home," she said. "He got back sooner than he expected. I guess the best thing would be to drive me over there. I suppose I'll have to go to Manistique for an X ray."

Link put the car in reverse, backed around, and started down the trail toward the road.

Two hours later he and Charley Horse sat in the waiting room of the hospital, waiting to learn just what had happened to Harriet's wrist.

"A man named Olson told me Aunt Harriet was an expert wildlife photographer and that she took a lot of pictures that were used in booklets and films," Link said.

"She was one of the best," Charley said. "A great photographer and she knew the woods. She would go anywhere at any time to get a picture. She went out once on snowshoes and stayed out several days to get pictures of moose in winter."

"How come you never told me about her being such

a good photographer, and an expert on sandhill cranes too?" Link asked.

Charley Horse's face was expressionless. "You never asked me," he said innocently.

"Huh," Link said in disgust.

"White man says huh, Indian says ugh," Charley said with a grin. "Means the same."

"This man Olson mentioned some bear pictures," Link said.

"Yes, while she was getting pictures of the bear, the bear almost got her," Charley said. "I saw those. She wrecked her camera getting away."

"Why does that man Sutcliffe hate her so?" Link asked. "He said she was a meddling busybody."

"Oh, you met old Sutcliffe, did you?" Charley asked.

"I certainly did," Link said. "And once is enough."

"His grandfather used to own thousands of acres back in the lumbering days," Charley explained. "It was all sold off or they lost it. All the family had left was some land around that camp. Then this Sutcliffe showed up from some place and began living in one of the old buildings. He talked big about how he was going to buy back all the timberland that had once belonged to the company. There was one big tract that belonged to some man in Detroit. Your aunt persuaded this man to give it or sell it cheaply to the Seney Wildlife Refuge. Sutcliffe thinks he could have bought it otherwise. I doubt if he had money enough in any case, but he thinks your aunt interfered. And I guess she would interfere if she thought she could keep land from being stripped the way it once was. They put in some dikes, and there is a big marsh on much of that land now. There are thousands of Canada geese breeding there."

"That's what he meant when he said she was more interested in geese than people," Link said with a grin.

Harriet appeared half an hour later. Her right wrist was in a plaster cast and her arm in a sling.

"It's not as bad as it looks," she said cheerfully. "It was a simple clean break, and the doctor says it should heal nicely."

"What do want to do now?" Charley asked. "Go back to the cabin?"

"I've been thinking about that," Harriet said.

Link had been thinking too. For weeks he had had just one idea—to get a picture of a sandhill crane. Then he would be free to catch the next plane back to New Jersey and to civilization. Well, he had succeeded. He finally had his pictures. But he couldn't leave now, not while Harriet had a broken wrist. It was as much out of the question as it would have been for her not to come to his rescue when he had been marooned on the island.

She had broken her wrist trying to keep his Uncle Al's camera from falling in the water, but even if there had been no accident, he wasn't certain he wanted to leave now. He was still homesick in a way, but it didn't bother him the way it had. He would like to see his mother, but she was planning on coming up to see him. He would enjoy showing her his woods and his island. It was funny how he thought of them as "his" now. Maybe he could take her out to the island and they could cook lunch there. It wouldn't be like one of her meals, but she would get a big thrill out of it.

"I suppose it will be five or six weeks before I can do much with my left hand," Harriet said. "I think the best thing is to go back to Melton. Do you suppose you could find someone I could pay to drive us down, Charley?"

"I think so if that is what you want," Charley replied.

"I think we ought to stay right here," Link said. "If you think you should go see your regular doctor or would be better off in Melton, that's a different matter. But I think you'd enjoy it more here, and I can do the cooking and whatever needs to be done at the cabin. And we have that fawn."

"You have your pictures of the sandhill cranes," Harriet reminded him.

"Yes, but there's a lot more pictures I'd like to take," Link said truthfully. "And right now I've got Uncle Al's camera equipment and an expert handy who can tell me about photographing animals and making film-strips. I don't know when I'll ever have that combination again."

Harriet smiled. "The cabin will be here, I'll be glad to work with you any time, and if you have the interest, cameras can always be found. But if you really feel like staying on, I can't think of anything that would please me more."

"I'd like to draw some of those crazy waterbirds, too," Link said.

"I'm suddenly very hungry," Harriet said. "None of us have had any dinner. I think we ought to go some place and have a good dinner to celebrate."

"That's a great idea," Link said. "I could eat a horse."

Harriet and Charley got in the front seat, and Link climbed in back. What he would really have liked was one of his mother's homecooked meals, but you couldn't have everything, it seemed. At least not all at one time and place. He would settle for a nice thick steak. He would really like to go home, but he wanted to stay too. Well, if he stayed another month, it would seem even better when he did get back. He remembered the Sunday dinner when they had all been so startled when he had mentioned going to Michigan for the summer. None of them had had any idea what he would get into, least of all himself. He might come back next summer. He might even study wildlife management or some sort of conservation when he went to college. It was crazy how one thing led to another. Uncle Albert had no idea what he had started when he had asked him to search for a sandhill crane.

ABOUT THE AUTHOR

KEITH ROBERTSON was born in Iowa and grew up on farms and in small towns in the Midwest. His family moved a great deal, and at one time or another they lived in Kansas, Oklahoma, Minnesota, Wisconsin, and Missouri. After graduation from high school, he served for two years in the Navy and then entered the United States Naval Academy at Annapolis.

When World War II began, Mr. Robertson went into the Navy as a reserve officer and served for five years on a destroyer, in both the Atlantic and the Pacific.

Mr. Robertson has written many popular books for young people, including *The Money Machine* and *The Year of the Jeep*. He is probably best known as the creator of the irrepressible Henry Reed. Two of these books, *Henry Reed, Inc.* and *Henry Reed's Baby-Sitting Service*, have won the William Allen White Children's Book Award.

Mr. Robertson and his wife live on a small farm in central New Jersey.